DREAM
SNAKE
Vonda N. McIntyre

ALFRED HITCHCOCK PRESENTS

STORIES NOT FOR THE NERVOUS

A DELL BOOK

The author gratefully acknowledges
the invaluable assistance of Robert Arthur
in the preparation of this volume

Published by
DELL PUBLISHING CO., INC.
750 Third Avenue
New York, N. Y. 10017

For information, address Random House, Inc.
Dell ® TM 681510, Dell Publishing Co., Inc.
Reprinted by arrangement with
Random House, Inc.
New York, New York
Printed in Canada
Previous Dell Edition #8288
New Dell Edition
First printing—September 1971

Acknowledgments

To The Future, by Ray Bradbury. Copyright, 1950, by Ray Bradbury. Reprinted by permission of The Harold Matson Company, Inc.

River of Riches, by Gerald Kersh. Reprinted by permission of Collins-Knowlton-Wing, Inc. Copyright © 1958, by The Curtis Publishing Company.

Levitation, by Joseph Payne Brennan. Copyright © 1958 by Joseph Payne Brennan. Reprinted by permission of Arkham House and the Scott Meredith Literary Agency, Inc.

Miss Winters and the Wind, by Christine Noble Govan. Reprinted by permission of the author. Copyright, 1946, by Creative Age Press, Inc.

The Man With Copper Fingers, by Dorothy L. Sayers. Reprinted from *Lord Peter Views The Body* by permission of A. Watkins, Inc. Copyright, 1928, by Anthony Fleming, renewed © copyright, 1956, by Anthony Fleming.

Twenty Friends of William Shaw, by Raymond E. Banks. Reprinted by permission of the author and *Mike Shayne Mystery Magazine.* © Copyright, 1960, by Raymond E. Banks.

The Other Hangman, by Carter Dickson. From *The Department of Queer Complaints,* by Carter Dickson. Copyright, 1940, by William Morrow and Company, Inc. Reprinted by permission of William Morrow and Company, Inc.

Don't Look Behind You, by Frederic Brown. Copyright, 1947, 1953, by Frederic Brown. Reprinted by permission of the author and the author's agent, the Scott Meredith Literary Agency, Inc. Originally appeared in *Ellery Queen's Mystery Magazine.*

No Bath For the Browns, by Margot Bennet. Reprinted by permission of David Higham Associates, Ltd., London. Copyright, 1944, by Margot Bennet.

The Uninvited, by Michael Gilbert. Reprinted by permission of the author. Copyright © 1960, by Popular Publications, Inc.

Dune Roller, by Julian May. Reprinted by permission of The

Conde Nast Publications Inc. Originally appeared in ASTOUNDING SCIENCE FICTION (now ANALOG *Science Fiction—Science Fact*). Copyright © 1951, by Julian May Dikty.
The Dog Died First, by BRUNO FISCHER. Reprinted by permission of the author and his agent, August Lenniger. Copyright, 1949, by Bruno Fischer.
The Substance of Martyrs, by WILLIAM SAMBROT. Reprinted by permission of the author. Copyright © 1963, by William Sambrot.

Contents

TO THE FUTURE	Ray Bradbury	9
RIVER OF RICHES	Gerald Kersh	24
THE MAN WITH COPPER FINGERS *(novelette)*	Dorothy L. Sayers	37
LEVITATION	Joseph Payne Brennan	56
MISS WINTERS AND THE WIND	Christine Noble Govan	61
THE DOG DIED FIRST *(novelette)*	Bruno Fischer	67
THE TWENTY FRIENDS OF WILLIAM SHAW	Raymond E. Banks	89
THE OTHER HANGMAN	Carter Dickson	98
DUNE ROLLER *(novelette)*	Julian May	112
NO BATH FOR THE BROWNS	Margot Bennet	154
THE UNINVITED	Michael Gilbert	157
THE SUBSTANCE OF MARTYRS	William Sambrot	168
DON'T LOOK BEHIND YOU	Frederic Brown	176

A BRIEF MESSAGE FROM OUR SPONSOR

The title of this volume is *Stories* Not *for the Nervous.* There are those who will argue that this title could apply to any of the various tomes of terror, sagas of suspense, or groupings of grue which I have, from time to time, gathered together for the delectation of my readers. And indeed the point is well taken.

For I am not a man to cater to the nervous. If you are in the habit of chewing your fingernails, jumping from your chair when a door slams, or swooning when someone playfully shouts "Boo!" in your ear, I have only two words of advice—pass on.

If, however, you have nerves which are under good control, nerves which are pleasantly tickled by a touch of terror or agreeably stimulated by a *soupçon* of suspense, then I invite you to join me.

Take a seat, any seat, and start wherever you wish. Break for an intermission whenever you choose and return when you are ready. Informality rules in your enjoyment of this smörgåsbord of stories. There is, I think, something for every taste.

Except, that is, for the nervous.

And now my sixty seconds are up.

ALFRED HITCHCOCK

To the Future

RAY BRADBURY

The fireworks sizzled across the cool-tiled square, banged against adobe café walls, then rushed on hot wires to bash the high church tower, while a fiery bull ran about the plaza chasing boys and laughing men. It was a spring night in Mexico in the year 1938.

Mr. and Mrs. William Travis stood on the edge of the yelling crowd, smiling. The bull charged. Ducking, the man and wife ran, fire pelting them, past the brass band that pulsed out vast rhythms of "La Paloma." The bull passed, a framework of bamboo and gunpowder, carried lightly on the shoulders of a charging Mexican.

"I've never enjoyed myself so much in my life," gasped Susan Travis, stopping.

"It's terrific," said William.

"It will go on, won't it? I mean our trip?"

He patted his breast pocket. "I've enough traveler's checks for a lifetime. Enjoy yourself. Forget it. They'll never find us."

"Never?"

Now someone hurled giant firecrackers from the bell tower.

The bull was dead. The Mexican lifted its framework from his shoulders. Children clustered to touch the magnificent papier-mâché animal.

"Let's examine the bull," said William.

As they walked past the café entrance, Susan saw the strange man looking out at them, a white man in a white suit, with a thin, sunburned face. His eyes coldly watched them as they walked.

She would never have noticed him if it had not been for the bottles at his immaculate elbow; a fat bottle of crème de menthe, a clear bottle of vermouth, a flagon of cognac, and seven others bottles of assorted liqueurs; and, at his fingertips, ten small half-filled glasses from which, without taking his eyes off the street, he sipped, occasionally squinting, pressing his thin mouth shut upon the savor. In his free hand a thin Havana cigar smoked, and on a chair stood twenty cartons of Turkish cigarettes, six boxes of cigars and some packaged colognes.

"Bill—" whispered Susan.

"Take it easy," William said. "That man's nobody."

"I saw him in the plaza this morning."

"Don't look back, keep walking, examine the papier-mâché bull—here, that's it, ask questions."

"Do you think he's from the Searchers?"

"They *couldn't* follow us!"

"They might!"

"What a nice bull," said William pleasantly to the man who owned it.

"He couldn't have followed us back through two hundred years, could he?"

"Watch yourself!" said William.

She swayed. He crushed her elbow tightly, steering her away.

"Don't faint." He smiled to make it look good. "You'll be all right. Let's go right in that café, drink in front of him, so if he *is* what we think he is, he won't suspect."

"No, I couldn't."

"We've *got* to—come on now. And so I said to David, that's *ridiculous!*" He spoke this last in a loud voice as they went up the café steps.

We are here, thought Susan. Who are we? Where are we going? What do we fear? Start at the beginning, she told herself, holding to her sanity, as she felt the adobe floor underfoot.

My name is Ann Kristen, my husband's name is Roger, we were born in the year 2155 A.D. And we lived in a world that was evil. A world that was like a great ship pulling away from the shore of sanity and civilization, roaring its black horn in the night, taking two billion people with it, whether they wanted to go or not, to death, to fall over the edge of the earth and the sea into radioactive flame and madness.

They walked into the café. The man was staring at them. A phone rang.

The phone startled Susan. She remembered a phone

ringing two hundred years in the future, on that blue April morning in 2155, and herself answering it:

"Ann, this is René! Have you heard? I mean about Travel In Time, Incorporated? Trips to Rome in 21 B.C., trips to Napoleon's Waterloo, any time, anyplace!"

"René, you're joking."

"No. Clinton Smith left this morning for Philadelphia in 1776. Travel In Time, Inc., arranges everything. Costs money. But *think*, to actually *see* the burning of Rome, to see Kublai Khan, Moses and the Red Sea! You've probably got an ad in your tube-mail now."

She had opened the suction mail-tube and there was the metal foil advertisement:

ROME AND THE BORGIAS!
THE WRIGHT BROTHERS AT
KITTY HAWK!

Travel In Time, Inc., can costume you, put you in a crowd during the assassination of Lincoln or Caesar! We guarantee to teach you any language you need to move freely in any civilization, in any year, without friction. Latin, Greek, ancient American colloquial. Take your vacation in TIME *as well as Place!*

René's voice was buzzing on the phone. "Tom and I leave for 1492 tomorrow. They're arranging for Tom to sail with Columbus—isn't it amazing?"

"Yes," murmured Ann, stunned. "What does the government say about this Time Machine Company?"

"Oh, the police have an eye on it. Afraid people might evade the draft, run off and hide in the Past. Everyone has to leave a security bond behind, his house and belongings, to guarantee return. After all, the war's on."

"Yes, the war," murmured Ann. "The war."

Standing there, holding the phone, she had thought: Here is the chance my husband and I have talked and prayed over for so many years. We don't like this world of 2155. We want to run away from his work at the bomb factory—from my position with disease-culture units. Perhaps there is some chance for us, to escape, to run for centuries into a wild country of years where they will never find us and bring us back to burn our books, censor our thoughts, scald our minds with fear, march us, scream at us with radios. . . .

The phone rang.

They were in Mexico in the year 1938.

She looked at the stained café wall.

Good workers for the Future State were allowed vacations into the Past to escape fatigue. And so she and her husband had moved back into 1938. They took a room in New York City, and enjoyed the theaters and the Statue of Liberty which still stood green in the harbor. And on the third day, they had changed their clothes and their names, and flown off to hide in Mexico.

"It *must* be him," whispered Susan, looking at the stranger seated at the table. "Those cigarettes, the cigars, the liquor. They give him away. Remember *our* first night in the Past?"

A month ago, on their first night in New York, before their flight, they had tasted all the strange drinks, bought odd foods, perfumes, cigarettes of ten dozen rare brands, for they were scarce in the Future, where war was everything. So they had made fools of themselves, rushing in and out of stores, salons, tobacconists', going up to their room to get wonderfully ill.

And now here was this stranger doing likewise, doing a thing that only a man from the Future would do, who had been starved for liquors and cigarettes too many years.

Susan and William sat and ordered a drink.

The stranger was examining their clothes, their hair, their jewelry, the way they walked and sat.

"Sit easily," said William under his breath. "Look as if you've worn this clothing style all your life."

"We should never have tried to escape."

"My God," said William. "He's coming over. Let me do the talking."

The stranger bowed before them. There was the faintest tap of heels knocking together. Susan stiffened. That military sound—unmistakable as that certain ugly rap on your door at midnight.

"Mr. Kristen," said the stranger, "you did not pull up your pant legs when you sat down."

William froze. He looked at his hands lying on either leg, innocently. Susan's heart was beating swiftly.

"You've got the wrong person," said William, quickly. "My name's not Krisler."

"Kristen," corrected the stranger.

"I'm William Travis," said William. "And I don't see what my pant legs have to do with you."

"Sorry." The stranger pulled up a chair. "Let us say I thought I knew you because you did *not* pull your trousers up. Everyone does. If they don't the trousers bag quickly. I am a long way from home, Mr.—Travis—and in need of company. My name is Simms."

"Mr. Simms, we appreciate your loneliness, but we're tired. We're leaving for Acapulco tomorrow."

"A charming spot. I was just there, looking for some friends of mine.

"They are somewhere. I shall find them yet. Oh, is the lady a bit sick?"

"Good night, Mr. Simms."

They started out the door, William holding Susan's arm firmly. They did not look back when Mr. Simms called. "Oh, just one other thing." He paused and then slowly spoke the words:

"Twenty-one fifty-five A.D."

Susan shut her eyes and felt the earth falter under her. She kept going, into the fiery plaza, seeing nothing. . . .

They locked the door of their hotel room. And then she was crying and they were standing in the dark, and the room tilted under them. Far away, firecrackers exploded, there was laughter in the plaza.

"What a damned, loud nerve," said William. "Him sitting there, looking us up and down like animals, smoking his damn cigarettes, drinking his drinks. I should have killed him then!" His voice was nearly hysterical. "He even had the nerve to use his real name to us. The Chief of the Searchers. And the thing about my pant legs. I should have pulled them up when I sat. It's an automatic gesture of this day and age. When I didn't do it, it set me off from the others. It made *him* think: Here's a man who never wore pants, a man used to breech-uniforms and Future styles. I could kill myself for giving us away!"

"No, no, it was my walk, these high heels, that did it. Our haircuts, so new, so fresh. Everything about us odd and uneasy."

William turned on the light. "He's still testing us. He's not positive of us, not completely. We can't run out on him, then. We can't make him certain. We'll go to Acapulco, leisurely."

"Maybe he *is* sure of us, but is just playing."

"I wouldn't put it past him. He's got all the time in the world. He can dally here if he wants, and bring us back to the Future sixty seconds after we left it. He might keep us wondering for days, laughing at us, before he acted."

Susan sat on the bed, wiping the tears from her face, smelling the old smell of charcoal and incense.

"They won't make a scene, will they?"

"They won't dare. They'll have to get us alone to put us in the Time Machine and send us back."

"There's a solution then," she said. "We'll never be alone, we'll always be in crowds."

Footsteps sounded outside their locked door.

They turned out the light and undressed in silence. The footsteps went away.

Susan stood by the window looking down at the plaza in the darkness. "So that building there is a church?"

"Yes."

"I've often wondered what a church looked like. It's been so long since anyone saw one. Can we visit it tomorrow?"

"Of course. Come to bed."

They lay in the dark room.

Half an hour later, their phone rang. She lifted the receiver.

"Hello?"

"The rabbits may hide in the forest," said a voice, "but a fox can always find them."

She replaced the receiver and lay back straight and cold in the bed.

Outside, in the year 1938, a man played three tunes upon a guitar, one following another. . . .

During the night, she put her hand out and almost touched the year 2155. She felt her fingers slide over cool spaces of time, as over a corrugated surface, and she heard the insistent thump of marching feet, a million bands playing a million military tunes. She saw the fifty thousand rows of disease-culture in their aseptic glass tubes, her hand reaching out to them at her work in that huge factory in the Future. She saw the tubes of leprosy, bubonic, typhoid, tuberculosis. She heard the great explosion and saw her hand burned to a wrinkled plum, felt it recoil from a concussion so immense that the world was lifted and let fall, and all the buildings broke and people hemorrhaged and lay silent. Great volcanoes, machines, winds, avalanches slid down to silence and she awoke, sobbing, in the bed, in Mexico, many years away . . .

In the early morning, drugged with the single hour's sleep they had finally been able to obtain, they awoke to the sound of loud automobiles in the street. Susan peered down from the iron balcony at a small crowd of eight people only now emerging, chattering, yelling, from trucks and cars with red lettering on them. A crowd of Mexicans had followed the trucks.

"Qué pasa?" Susan called to a little boy.

The boy replied.

Susan turned back to her husband. "An American motion picture company, here on location."

"Sounds interesting." William was in the shower. "Let's watch them. I don't think we'd better leave today. We'll try to lull Simms."

For a moment, in the bright sun, she had forgotten that somewhere in the hotel, waiting, was a man smoking a thousand cigarettes, it seemed. She saw the eight loud, happy Americans below and wanted to call to them: "Save me, hide me, help me! I'm from the year 2155!"

But the words stayed in her throat. The functionaries of Travel In Time, Inc., were not foolish. In your brain, before you left on your trip, they placed a psychological block. You could tell no one your true time or birthplace, nor could you reveal any of the Future to those in the Past. The Past and the Future must be protected from each other. Only with this hindrance were people allowed to travel unguarded through the ages. The Future most be protected from any change brought about by her people traveling in the Past. Even if Susan wanted to with all of her heart, she could not tell any of those happy people below in the plaza who she was, or what her predicament had become.

"What about breakfast?" said William.

Breakfast was being served in the immense dining room. Ham and eggs for everyone. The place was full of tourists. The film people entered, all eight of them, six men and two women, giggling, shoving chairs about. And Susan sat near them feeling the warmth and protection they offered, even when Mr. Simms came down the lobby stairs, smoking his Turkish cigarette with great intensity. He nodded at them from a distance, and Susan nodded back, smiling, because he couldn't do anything to them here, in front of eight film people and twenty other tourists.

"Those actors," said William. "Perhaps I could hire two of them, say it was a joke, dress them in our clothes, have them drive off in our car, when Simms is in such a spot where he can't see their faces. If two people pretending to be us could lure him off for a few hours, we might make it to Mexico City. It would take him years to find us there!"

"Hey!"

A fat man, with liquor on his breath, leaned on their table.

"American tourists!" he cried. "I'm so sick of seeing Mexicans, I could kiss you!" He shook their hands. "Come on, eat with us. Misery loves company. I'm Misery, this is Miss Gloom, and Mr. and Mrs. Do-We-Hate-Mexico! We all hate it. But we're here for some preliminary shots for a damn film. The rest of the crew arrives tomorrow. My name's Joe Melton, I'm a director, and if this ain't a hell of a country—funerals in the streets, people dying—come on, move over, join the party, cheer us up!"

Susan and William were both laughing.

"Am I funny?" Mr. Melton asked the immediate world.

"Wonderful!" Susan moved over.

Mr. Simms was glaring across the dining room at them. She made a face at him.

Mr. Simms advanced among the tables.

"Mr. and Mrs. Travis!" he called. "I thought we were breakfasting together, alone?"

"Sorry," said William.

"Sit down, pal," said Mr. Melton. "Any friend of theirs is a pal of mine."

Mr. Simms sat. The film people talked loudly and while they talked, Mr. Simms said, quietly, "I hope you slept well."

"Did you?"

"I'm not used to spring mattresses," replied Mr. Simms, wryly. "But there are compensations. I stayed up half the night trying new cigarettes and foods. Odd, fascinating. A whole new spectrum of sensation, these ancient vices."

"We don't know what you're talking about," said Susan.

Simms laughed. "Always the play acting. It's no use. Nor is this stratagem of crowds. I'll get you alone soon enough. I'm immensely patient."

"Say," Mr. Melton broke in, "is this guy giving you any trouble?"

"It's all right."

"Say the word and I'll give him the bum's rush."

Melton turned back to yell at his associates. In the laughter, Mr. Simms went on: "Let us come to the point. It took me a month of tracing you through towns and cities to find you, and all of yesterday to be sure of you. If you come with me quietly, I might be able to get you off with no punishment—if you agree to go back to work on the Hydrogen-Plus bomb."

"We don't know what you're talking about."

"Stop it!" cried Simms, irritably. "Use your intelligence! You know we can't let you get away with this escape. Other people in the year 2155 might get the same idea and do the same. We need people."

"To fight your wars," said William.

"Bill!"

"It's all right, Susan. We'll talk on his terms now. We can't escape."

"Excellent," said Simms. "Really, you've both been incredibly romantic, running away from responsibilities."

"Running away from horror."

"Nonsense. Only a war."

"What are you guys talking about?" asked Mr. Melton.

Susan wanted to tell him. But you could only speak in generalities. The psychological block in your mind allowed that. Generalities, such as Simms and William were now discussing.

"Only *the* war," said William. "Half the world dead of leprosy bombs!"

"Nevertheless," Simms pointed out, "the inhabitants of the Future resent you two hiding on a tropical isle, as it were, while they drop off the cliff into hell. Death loves death, not life. Dying people love to know that others die with them; it is a comfort to learn you are not alone in the kiln, in the grave. I am the guardian of their collective resentment against you two."

"Look at the guardian of resentments!" said Mr. Melton to his companions.

"The longer you keep me waiting, the harder it will go for you. We need you on the bomb project, Mr. Travis. Return now—no torture. Later, we'll force you to work and after you've finished the bomb, we'll try a number of complicated new devices on you, sir."

"I've got a proposition," said William. "I'll come back with you, if my wife stays here alive, safe, away from that war."

Mr. Simms debated. "All right. Meet me in the plaza in ten mintues. Pick me up in your car. Drive me to a deserted country spot. I'll have the Travel Machine pick us up there where there won't be any witnesses."

"Bill!" Susan held his arm tightly.

"Don't argue." He looked over at her. "It's settled." To Simms: "One thing. Last night, you could have got in our room and kidnapped us. Why didn't you?"

"Shall we say that I was enjoying myself?" replied Mr. Simms languidly, sucking his new cigar. "I hate giving up this wonderful atmosphere, this sun, this vacation. I regret leaving behind the wine and the cigarettes. Oh, how I regret it. The plaza then, in ten minutes. Your wife will be protected and may stay here as long as she wishes. Say your good-byes."

Mr. Simms arose and walked out.

"There goes Mr. Big-Talk!" yelled Mr. Melton at the departing gentleman. He turned and looked at Susan. "Hey. Someone's crying. Breakfast's no time for people to cry, now *is* it?"

At nine-fifteen, Susan stood on the balcony of their room, gazing down at the plaza. Mr. Simms was seated there, his neat legs crossed, on a delicate bronze bench. Biting the tip from a cigar, he lighted it tenderly.

Susan heard the throb of a motor, and far up the street, out of a garage and down the cobbled hill, slowly, came William in his car.

The car picked up speed. Thirty, now forty, now fifty miles an hour. Chickens scattered before it.

Mr. Simms took off his white Panama hat and mopped his pink forehead, put his hat back on, and then saw the car.

It was rushing sixty miles an hour, straight on for the plaza.

"William!" screamed Susan.

The car hit the low plaza curb, thundering, jumped up, sped across the tiles toward the green bench where Mr. Simms now dropped his cigar, shrieked, flailed his hands, and was hit by the car. His body flew up and up in the air, and down, crazily, into the street.

On the far side of the plaza, one front wheel broken, the car stopped. People were running.

Susan went in and closed the balcony doors.

They came down the Official Palace steps together, arm in arm, their faces pale, at twelve noon.

"Adiós, señor," said the mayor behind them. *"Señora."*

They stood in the plaza where the crowd was pointing at the blood.

"Will they want to see you again?" asked Susan.

"No, we went over and over it. It was an accident. I lost control of the car. I wept for them. God knows I had to get my relief out somewhere. I *felt* like weeping. I hated to kill him. I've never wanted to do anything like that in my life."

"They won't prosecute you?"

"They talked about it, but no. I talked faster. They believe me. It was an accident. It's over."

"Where will we go? Mexico City?"

"The car's in the repair shop. It'll be ready at four this afternoon. Then we'll get the hell out."

"Will we be followed? Was Simms working alone?"

"I don't know. We'll have a little head start on them, I think."

The film people were coming out of the hotel as they approached. Mr. Melton hurried up, scowling. "Hey, I heard what happened. Too bad. Everything okay now? Want to get your minds off it? We're doing some preliminary shots up the street. You want to watch, you're welcome. Come on, do you good."

They went.

They stood on the cobbled street while the film camera was being set up. Susan looked at the road leading down and away, at the highway going to Acapulco and the sea, past pyramids and ruins and little adobe towns with yellow walls, blue walls, purple walls and flaming bougainvillaea. She thought: We shall take the roads, travel in clusters and crowds, in markets, in lobbies, bribe police to sleep near, keep double locks, but always the crowds, never alone again, always afraid the next person who passes might be another Simms. Never knowing if we've tricked and lost the Searchers. And always up ahead, in the Future, they'll wait for us to be brought back, waiting with their bombs to burn us and disease to rot us, and their police to tell us to roll over, turn around, jump through the hoop. And so we'll keep running through the forest, and we'll never ever stop or sleep well again in our lives.

A crowd gathered to watch the film being made. And Susan watched the crowd and the streets.

"Seen anyone suspicious?"

"No. What time is it?"

"Three o'clock. The car should be almost ready."

The test film was finished at three forty-five. They all walked down to the hotel, talking. William paused at the garage. "The car'll be ready at six," he said, coming out.

"But no later than that?"

"It'll be ready, don't worry."

In the hotel lobby they looked around for other men traveling alone, men who resembled Mr. Simms, men with new haircuts and too much cigarette smoke and cologne smell about them, but the lobby was empty. Going up the stairs, Mr. Melton said, "Well, it's been a long, hard day. Who'd like to put a header on it. Martini? Beer?"

"Maybe one."

The whole crowd pushed into Mr. Melton's room and the drinking began.

"Watch the time," said William.

Time, thought Susan, if only they had time. All she wanted was to sit in the plaza all of a long, bright day in spring, with not a worry or a thought, with the sun on her face and arms, her eyes closed, smiling at the warmth—and never move, but just sleep in the Mexican sun . . .

Mr. Melton opened the champagne.

"To a very beautiful lady, lovely enough for films," he said, toasting Susan. "I might even give you a test."

She laughed.

"I mean it," said Melton. "You're very nice. I could make you a movie star."

"And take me to Hollywood?"

"Get the hell out of Mexico, sure!"

Susan glanced at William, and he lifted an eyebrow and nodded. It would be a change of scene, clothing, locale, name perhaps, and they would be traveling with eight other people, a good shield against any interference from the future.

"It sounds wonderful," said Susan.

She was feeling the champagne now, the afternoon was slipping by, the party was whirling about her, she felt safe and good and alive and truly happy for the first time in many years.

"What kind of film would my wife be good for?" asked William, refilling his glass.

Melton appraised Susan. The party stopped laughing and listened.

"Well, I'd like to do a story of suspense," said Melton. "A story of a man and wife, like yourselves."

"Go on."

"Sort of a war story, maybe," said the director, examining the color of his drink against the sunlight.

Susan and William waited.

"A story about a man and wife who live in a little house on a little street in the year 2155, maybe," said Melton. "This is ad lib, understand. But this man and wife are faced with a terrible war, Super-Plus Hydrogen bombs, censorship, death, in that year and—here's the gimmick—they escape into the past, followed by a man who they think is evil, but who is only trying to show them what their Duty is."

William dropped his glass to the floor.

Mr. Melton continued. "And this couple take refuge with a group of film people whom they learn to trust. Safety in numbers, they say to themselves."

Susan felt herself slip down into a chair. Everyone was watching the director. He took a little sip of wine. "Ah, that's a fine wine. Well, this man and woman, it seems, don't realize how important they are to the future. The man, especially, is the keystone to a new bomb metal. So the Searchers, let's call them, spare no trouble or expense to find, capture, and take home the man and wife, once they get them totally alone, in a hotel room, where no one can see. Strategy. The Searchers work alone, or in groups of eight. One trick or another will do it. Don't you think it would make a wonderful film, Susan? Don't you, Bill?" He finished his drink.

Susan sat with her eyes straight ahead.

"Have a drink?" said Mr. Melton.

William's gun was out and fired three times, and one of the men fell, and the others ran forward. Susan screamed. A hand was clamped to her mouth. Now the gun was on the floor and William was struggling with the men holding him.

Mr. Melton said, "Please," standing there where he had stood, blood showing on his fingers. "Let's not make matters worse."

Someone pounded on the hall door.

"Let me in!"

"The manager," said Mr. Melton, dryly. He jerked his head. "Everyone, let's move!"

"Let me in. I'll call the police!"

Susan and William looked at each other quickly, and then at the door.

"The manager wishes to come in," said Mr. Melton. "Quick!"

A camera was carried forward. From it shot a blue light which encompassed the room instantly. It widened out and the people of the party vanished, one by one.

"Quickly!"

Outside the window in the instant before she vanished, Susan saw the green land and the purple and yellow and blue and crimson walls and the cobbles flowing like a river, a man upon a burro riding into the warm hills, a boy drinking orange pop. She could feel the sweet liquid in her throat; she could see a man standing under a cool plaza tree with a guitar, could feel her hand upon the strings. And, far away, she could see the sea, the blue and tender sea; she could feel it roll her over and take her in.

And then she was gone. Her husband was gone.

The door burst wide. The manager and his staff rushed in.

The room was empty.

"But they were just here! I saw them come in, and now —gone!" cried the manager. "The windows are covered with iron grating; they couldn't get out that way!" . . .

In the late afternoon, the priest was summoned and they

opened the room again and aired it out, and had him sprinkle holy water through each corner and give it his cleansing.

"What shall we do with these?" asked the charwoman.

She pointed to the closet, where there were sixty-seven bottles of chartreuse, cognac, *crème de cacao,* absinthe, vermouth, tequila, 106 cartons of Turkish cigarettes, and 198 yellow boxes of fifty-cent pure Havana-filler cigars. . . .

River of Riches

GERALD KERSH

About the man called Pilgrim there was a certain air of something gone stale. "Seedy" is the word for it, as applied to a human being. It was difficult to regard him except as a careful housewife regards a pot of homemade jam upon the surface of which she observes a patch of mildew. *Sweet but questionable*, she says to herself, *but it is a pity to waste it. Give it to the poor.* So, as it seemed to me, it was with Pilgrim.

He was curiously appealing to me in what looked like a losing fight against Skid Row, and maintained a haughty reserve when the bartender, detaining him as he abstractedly started to stroll out of MacAroon's Grill, said, "Daddle be a dollar-ten, doc."

Pilgrim slapped himself on the forehead, and beat himself about the pockets, and cried, "My wallet! I left it at home."

"Oh-oh," the bartender said, lifting the counter flap.

Then I said, "Here's the dollar-ten, Mike. Let the man go."

But Pilgrim would not go. He took me by the arm, and said in the old-fashioned drawling kind of Oxford accent, "No, but really, this is too kind! I'm afraid I can't reciprocate. As a fellow limey you will understand. One's position here becomes invidious. You see, I have only just now lost two fortunes, and am in the trough of the wave between the second and the third—which I assure you is not farther off than the middle of next month. I must get to Detroit. But allow me to introduce myself by the name by which I prefer to be known: John Pilgrim. Call me Jack. In honesty, I ought to tell you that this is not my real name. If some plague were to wipe out the male members of my family in a certain quarter of Middlesex, in England, I should be addressed very differently; and ride my horses, to boot. As matters stand, I am the younger son of a younger son, cast out with a few thousand pounds in my pocket, to make my fortune in Canada."

I asked, "Was that your first fortune?"

"Heavens, no! Man on the boat had an infallible system shooting dice. I arrived in Canada, sir, with four dollars and eighteen cents—and my clothes. I roughed it, I assure you. Clerk in a hardware store, dismissed on unjust suspicion of peculation; errand boy at a consulate, kicked out for what they called 'shaking down' an applicant for a visa, which was a lie; representative of a wine merchant, wrongly accused of drinking the samples. I went through the mill, I do assure you. And now I am offered a lucrative post in Detroit."

"Doing what?" I asked.

He said, "Checking things for a motor company."

"What things?"

"A word to the wise is sufficient. This is strictly hush-hush. Less said the better, what? But I can put you in the way of a few million dollars if you have time and money to spare."

"Pray do so," I said.

"I will. But not being a complete fool I will not be exact in my geography. Do you know Brazil? I know where there is a massive fortune in virgin gold in one of the tributaries of the Amazon. . . . Oh, dear, it really is a bitter fact that men with money who want some more insist on having the more before they lay out the less! Yet I tell you without the least reserve that I got about ten thousand ounces of pure gold out of the people who live by that river"

"How did you manage that?" I asked.

Pilgrim smiled at me, and said, "I dare say you have heard of the tocte nut? No? . . . Well, the tocte nut comes from Ecuador. It is something like an English walnut, only perfectly oval, almost. As in the case of the walnut, the kernel of the tocte nut resembles in its lobes, twists and convolutions, the human brain. It is bitter to eat, and is used generally by children for playing with, as we used to play with marbles.

"Ah, but this is in Ecuador. Go into Brazil, into a certain tributary of the Amazon, and I can show you a place where these nuts—or close relations of theirs—are taken very seriously indeed. The tribesmen do not call them tocte, but tictoc, and only adults play with these nuts in Brazil—

for extremely high stakes too. Fortunes—as they are counted in these wild parts—are won or lost on one game with the tictoc nuts. The savages have a saying there: '*Tic-toc* takes twenty years to learn.' To proceed: . . ."

From vicissitude to vicissitude is the destiny of the younger son (he said). I could, of course, have written to my elder brother for money. In fact I did. But he didn't answer. In the end, I shipped as cook on a freighter bound for South America. I suspect it was running guns. The crew was composed of the offscourings of Lapland, Finland, Iceland and San Francisco.

I jumped ship first opportunity, with nothing in my pockets but the papers of an oiler named Martinsen which I must have picked up by accident, and looked, as one does, for a fellow countryman. Luckily—I have the most astonishing luck—I overheard a man in a bar ordering whisky and soda without ice. Blood calls to blood. I was at his elbow in a trice.

He was a huge fellow, and was about to go to the place —which, if you'll forgive me, I won't mention—prospecting for rubies. Desirous of civilized company, he invited me to come along with him—said he would make it worth my while—offered me a share in the profits. He found the equipment, of course: quinine, rifles, trade goods, shotguns, soap and all that.

His idea was that, the market being good just then, if the worst came to the worst we might make our expenses out of snake skin and alligator hide. His name was Grimes, but he knew a gentleman when he saw one. But he was accident prone. Exploring mud for rubies, Grimes stood on a log to steady himself. The log came to life, opened a pair of jaws, and carried him off—an alligator, of course. They tell me that a mature alligator can, with his jaws, exert a pressure of nearly one thousand pounds' weight. It upset me, I don't mind telling you. Ever since then I have never been able to look at an alligator without disgust. They bring me bad luck.

The following morning I awoke to find my attendants all gone. They had paid themselves in trade goods, leaving me with only what I slept in—pajamas—plus a rifle, a bandoleer of .30-.30 cartridges, my papers and some dried beef.

Goodness only knows what might have happened to me

if I had not been rescued by cannibals—and jolly fine fellows they were too. Sportsmen, I assure you. They only ate women past marriageable age. They took me to their chief. I thought I was in a pretty sticky spot, at first, but he gave me some stew to eat—it was monkey, I hope—and while I ate I looked about me. Anyone could see with half an eye that the old gentleman wanted my rifle.

Now I reasoned as follows: I am outnumbered about two hundred and fifty to one by savages armed with spears and poisoned arrows. In the circumstances my rifle must be worse than useless. Better make a virtue of the inevitable and give it to him before he takes it away. Be magnanimous, Jack!

So, expressing delight at the flavor of the stew, I gave him the rifle and the bandoleer. He was overwhelmed with joy and gratitude and wanted to know what he could do for me. He offered me girls, more stew, necklaces of human teeth. I conveyed to him that I might prefer a few rubies. Heartbroken, he said that he had none of the red stones, only the green ones, and handed me a fistful of emeralds to the value, conservatively, of a thousand rifles at a hundred and twenty dollars apiece.

I thanked him politely, controlling my emotions as our sort of people are brought up to do. But he mistook my impassive air for disappointment. He was downcast for a moment or two. Then he brightened and said to me, "Wait. I have something that will make you very rich. It has made me chief. But now I am too old to play. I will give it to you."

Then he fumbled in what might laughingly be described as his clothes, and produced—guess what—a nut! Upon my word, a common nut, something like a walnut, but smooth and much larger in circumference at one end than at the other. Through years of handling, it had a wonderful patina, like very old bronze. "You know tictoc?" the old boy asked.

"I know tocte," I said. "It is a game played by children in Ecuador."

"You play?" he asked.

"Never. In Ecuador I have seen it played. In England we call it marbles."

"Of these places," said the chief, "I have never heard. Here, it is tictoc."

Then he went on to explain—it took all night—that the tictoc nut was not like other nuts. Everything, said the chief, everything could think a little. Even a leaf had sense enough to turn itself to the light. Even a rat. Even a woman. Sometimes, even a hard-shelled nut. Now when the world was made, the deuce of a long time ago, man having been created, there was a little intelligence left over for distribution. Woman got some. Rats got some. Leaves got some. Insects got some. In short, at last there was very little left.

Then the tictoc bush spoke up and begged, "A little for us?"

The answer came, "There are so many of you, and so little left to go around. But justice must be done. One in every ten million of you shall think with a man, and do his bidding. We have spoken."

So, the old geezer affirmed, the kernel of the tictoc nut came to resemble the human brain. Stroking his great knife, he assured me that he had many times seen one, and the resemblance was uncanny. Superficially, you understand.

To only one tictoc nut in ten million was vouchsafed the gift of thought. And the nuts, being very prolific, grew in the jungles in great profusion. Anyone who could find the ten-millionth nut, the thinking nut, was assured of good fortune, the old savage told me, because this nut would obey its master.

"Now play tictoc," he said.

I said, "But I don't know how."

He did not answer, but led me to a strip of ground stamped flat and level, and polished by innumerable feet. At one end someone had described a circle drawn with ocher. In this circle were arranged ten nuts in this pattern:

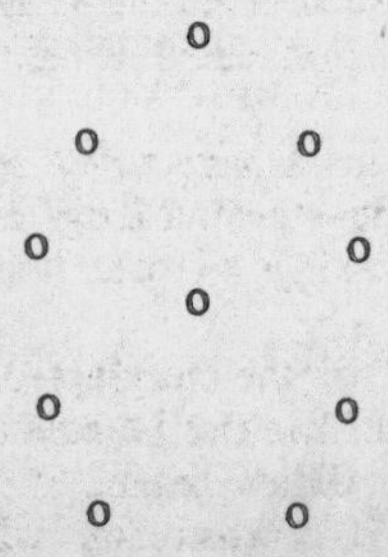

```
        o

    o       o

  o           o
        o

  o           o

    o       o
```

The object of the game was to knock the ten nuts out of the circle in the fewest possible shots. As a game, I should say that tictoc was much more difficult than pool, pyramids or snooker. You shot from a distance of about seven feet. It was a good player who could clear the circle in five shots; a remarkable one who could do it in four; a superlative one who could do it in three, flipping the oval tictoc nut with a peculiar twist of the thumb.

Several young fellows were playing, but more were betting their very loincloths on the champion, who had recently made a Three.

"Now," the old codger whispered, "rub the tictoc between your hands, breathe on it and shout without sound —shout at the back of your mind—telling it what to do. Challenge the champion. Stake your shirt."

The top of my pajamas could be no great loss. Furthermore, I had the emeralds, you know. So I took it off and offered my challenge. The young buck felt the cotton and put down against it a necklace of good nuggets, the largest of which was about as big as a grape.

He played first. On his first shot, out went five. Second, out went four. The last was easy. He had scored a Three.

And now it was my turn. Caressing my nut I said to it, without talking, "Now, old thing, show them what you can do. Try for a One, just to astonish the natives."

Without much hope, and with no skill at all, I flipped my nut. It seemed to stop halfway, gyrating. Everybody laughed, and my opponent reached for my pajama top—when, suddenly, my nut kind of shouldered its way forward into the circle, and with something devilishly like careful aim, spun its way into the ten and pushed them, one by one, beyond the bounds of the ring.

You never heard such a shout! I had broken a record. Picking my nut up, I caressed it and warmed it in my hand.

The chief said, "This I have never seen. Two, yes. One, no. I know what it is—the markings inside that nut must exactly match the markings of your brain. You are a lucky man."

Feeling the weight of the necklace I had won, I asked, "Is there any more stuff like this hereabout?"

He said no, they didn't regard it especially. The ex-champion had won it downstream, where they picked it out of the river bed and gave it to their women for ornaments. A string of your enemy's teeth meant something. But the yellow stuff was too soft and too heavy. "If you want it, take your tictoc nut and you can win as much of it as you can carry away—you and ten strong men."

I promised him that when I came back I would bring more guns and bullets, hatchets, knives, and all his heart could desire, if he would lend me a good canoe and the services of half a dozen sturdy men to paddle it, together with food and water. He agreed, and we took off.

In fine, I cleaned out that village and went on downstream with two war canoes, all loaded with gold and other valuables, such as garnets, emeralds, et cetera. I should have left it at that. But success had gone to my head.

On the way I stayed the night in the shack of a petty trader, a Portuguese, from whom I bought a whole suit of white-duck clothes, a couple of shirts, and pants and some other stuff. "Your fame has gone before you," he said, looking enviously at me and then at the gold nuggets I had paid him with. "They call you the Tictoc Man up and down the river. Now I happen to know that no white man can play tictoc—it takes twenty years to learn. How do you do it?"

I said, "A mere knack."

"Well, give me another nugget and I'll give you some good advice. . . . Thank you. My advice is, make straight for the big river, and so to the coast. Don't stop to play at the next village—there is only one—or you may regret it. The Esporco are the most villainous Indians in these parts. Don't push even your luck too far. Four ounces of gold, and I'll let you have a fine weapon, a revolver, all the way from Belgium."

The revolver I took, but not his advice, and we went on at dawn. In the late afternoon several canoes came out to meet us. My men spat and said, "Esporco, master—very bad."

"What, will they attack us?" I asked.

"No." They indicated that the Esporco Indian was the worst trickster and cheat in the Mato Grosso. But I fondled the tictoc nut, while observing that in every canoe sat a girl wearing a necklace of raw rubies, and little else. The men—big fellows, as Indians go—had an easy, cozy way with them, all smiles, no weapons, full of good humor.

They hailed me as Senhor Tictoc, while the girls threw flowers.

My leading paddler, the stroke, as it were, growled, "When Esporco bring flowers, keep your hand on your knife"—a savage version of *Timeo Danaos et dona ferentes.*

Still, I gave orders to land, and was received with wild delight. The chief ordered several young goats killed. I presented him with a sack of salt, which is highly prized thereabout. There was a banquet with a profusion of some slightly effervescent drink in the nature of the Mexican mescal, only lighter and breezier.

In a little while we started to talk business. I expressed interest in rubies. The chief said, "Those red things? But they are nothing." And, taking a magnificent necklace from one of the girls, he tossed it into the river—I was to learn, later, that he had a net there to catch it. "I have heard that you are interested in stones," said he, while I gaped like a fish. And he went away and came back with an uncut diamond of the Brazilian variety, as big as your two fists.

I displayed no emotion, but said, "Interesting. How much do you want for it?"

He said, "It has no price. I have been around, and know the value your people set on such stones. I also know—we all know on this river—what would happen if the news got about that there was gold, rubies, emeralds and diamonds hereabout. Your people would come down on us like jaguars, and drive us off the face of the earth. As it is, we have enough, we are contented, we regard such stuff as this as pretty for unmarried girls. No, my friend, it is not for sale. But I tell you what. It being a plaything, let us play for it. You have a great reputation as a tictoc player. As it happens, so have I. Now what have you to stake against this stone?"

"Three canoeloads of treasure," I said.

At this, one of his sons chimes in with, "Don't do it, father! The man is a wizard. All the river knows it. He has a thinking nut!"

Apparently tipsy, the chief shouted, "Silence, brat! There is no such thing. It is a superstition. Tictoc is a game of skill, and I am the best man on this river." He became angry. "Who questions my skill?"

Nobody did. The circle was made, the ten nuts arranged

at their proper distances. I begged my host to shoot first. There was a breathless hush as he went down on his knees and shot a perfect Two—at which there was a murmur of applause.

Then I stroked my nut and asked it for a One. Out it went, spinning like a little whirlwind, and a One it was.

It is etiquette, in the tictoc game, for the winner to pick up the fighting nuts and bring them back to the base. Loser shoots first. This time the chief shot a Three. I was feeling warm-hearted. Who wouldn't, if he was certain to win a diamond that would make the Koh-i-noor and the Cullinan diamonds look like stones in a fifty-dollar engagement ring? So I said to my nut, "This time, for the sport of the thing, get me a Five. But last shot we'll have another One and the best out of three games."

It did as it was bid, and I lost with a Five. The Chief much elated, got our nuts and handed me mine with grave courtesy. I shot with perfect confidence. Imagine my horror when, instead of moving with grace and deliberation, it reeled drunkenly forward and barely reached the periphery of the circle! I wondered, could that mescal-like stuff I had drunk have gone to its head through mine? Thinking with all my might, I shot again—and knocked one nut out of the ring. A third time, and I finished with an Eight.

The chief went to pick up our nuts. I was numb with grief. He handed me the nut I had played that last game with. I looked at it—and it was not my own!

Then the truth dawned on me. The old rascal had swapped nuts after the second game! Simple as that. But I kept my temper, because in a split second everybody had stopped laughing, and every man had produced a machete, an ax, a bow or spear. I said, "There is some mistake here, sir. This is not my tictoc nut."

"Then whose is it?"

"Yours. You are, no doubt inadvertently, holding mine in your hand. Give it back, if you please."

And driven beyond prudence, I made a grab at it. I was fast, but he was faster, and surprisingly strong. I, too, am tolerably strong in the fingers. We stood locked, hand to hand, for about twenty seconds. Then I heard and felt a sharp little crack. So did he, for he stood back, waving away his tribesmen who were closing in.

He held out his hand with dignity; it held the common

tictoc nut that he had palmed off on me. In my palm lay my own true nut, but split down the center, exposing the kernel.

I looked at it, fascinated. You know, I studied medicine once—might be in Harley Street by now, only there was a bureaucratic misunderstanding about four microscopes I borrowed. Silly old asses! I'd have got them out of pawn and put them back where I'd found them, as soon as my remittance came in. But no, they gave me the sack.

However, I have read some anatomy, and I solemnly swear that the kernel of my poor tictoc nut definitely and in detail resembled the human brain—convolutions, lobes, cerebrum, cerebellum, medulla—in every respect.

Most remarkable of all, when I touched it affectionately with my finger tip, it throbbed very faintly, and then lay still. Whereupon some of the virtue seemed to drain out of me, and I cried like a child.

But I pulled myself together and said, "Well, the bet is off. The game is null and void. Let me get my men together and push off."

Then, in the light of torches, I saw bundles on the shore —very familiar bundles.

"To save your men unnecessary exertion," the chief said, "I had them unload your canoes for you. I wish you no harm, but put it to you that you go quietly back where you belong. Come, you shall not go empty handed. Take as many small nuggets as your two hands can hold, and depart in peace. You overreached yourself. I would have given you the diamond for the thinking nut, and gladly, in fair exchange. But no, you had to cheat, to do bad trade, to bet on a sure thing. In this life, nothing is sure."

I said, holding out the revolver, "And what will you give me for this?"

"Oh, two double handfuls of gold."

"May I suggest three?"

"If you will allow me to test it first."

I did. He fired one shot into the dark. I took the gun back and said, "First, the gold."

Down by the river I took the liberty of scooping up a handful of heavy clay and filling up the barrel of that revolver. It would dry like brick. That old rogue would never play tictoc again.

But in burying the remains of my thinking nut, I had a

weird feeling that I was leaving behind a certain essential portion of myself. Gold and jewels I can get again. But that, never.

"So I got to the coast and took ship, as a passenger this time, on a heavy freighter bound for Tampa, Florida. What with one thing and another, I arrived with only a few nuggets left, which I keep as . . . I don't know, call it keepsakes. You have been very kind to me. Let me give you one—a very little one—and then I must be on my way. Have this one."

He dropped a heavy gold pellet on the wet table. It was not much larger than a pea, but shaped, or misshapen, beyond human conception. Fire and water had done that.

"Have it made into a tie pin," said Pilgrim.

"But I couldn't take a valuable thing like this," I cried, "without doing something for you in return!"

"Not a bit of it. We limeys must stick together, and I'm on my way to Detroit. About seven days from now, John Pilgrim, at Detroit's leading hotel, will find me. Help me on my way, if you like, but—" He shrugged.

"I have only ten dollars," I said, deeply moved by a certain sadness in Pilgrim's eyes. "You're welcome to that."

"You're very obliging. It shall be returned with interest."

"I must go now," I said.

"So must I," said he.

Marveling at the intricacies of the human mind, I walked until I found myself on Sixth Avenue, near West 46th Street, in which area congregate those who, with pitying smiles and a certain kind of shrug, can flaw a diamond carat by carat until you are ashamed to own it, and with a shake of the head depreciate a watch until it stops of its own accord. On impulse I went into a shop there and, putting down Pilgrim's nugget, asked what such a bit of gold might be worth.

His reply was, "Ya kiddin'? Tickle me so I'll laugh. What's the current price of printer's metal? . . . Worth? Kugel's Kute Novelties sell those twelve for fifty cents, mail order. I can get 'em for ya a dollar for two dozen. A teaspoonful lead, melt it and drop it in cold water. You can honestly advertise 'no two alike.' Gild 'em, and there's a nugget. A miniature gold brick. That manufacturer, so he puts out loaded dice 'for amusement only'—he sells 'em too. Seriously, did you buy this?"

I said, "Yes and no." But as I dropped the nugget into my pocket and turned to go, the shopman said, "Wait a minute, mister—it's a nice imitation and a good job of plating. Maybe I might give you a couple bucks for it!"

"Oh, no, you won't," I said, my suspicions aroused. I fondled the nugget in my pocket; it had the indescribable, authentic feel of real gold. As for that trick with melted lead and cold water, I suddenly remembered that I had played it myself about thirty years ago, with some broken toy soldiers, just for the sake of playing with fire. Recently-melted lead has a feel all its own, and is sharp at the edges. But my nugget felt old and worn.

"It could be, after forty years, for once I made a mistake," the man said. "Let's have another look."

But I went out, and visited another shop a few doors away: one of those double-fronted establishments, in the right-hand window of which, under a sign which says OLD GOLD BOUGHT, there lies a mess of pinchback bracelets, ancient watch chains, old false teeth and tie pins. In the other window, diamonds carefully carded and priced at anything between two thousand and fifteen thousand dollars. The proprietor, here, looked as if he were next door but one to the breadline.

I put down my nugget and said boldly, "How much for this?"

He scrutinized the nugget, put it in a balance and weighed it; then tested it on a jeweler's stone, with several kinds of acid. "Voigin gold," he said. "Where'd you get it?"

"A friend gave it to me."

"I wish I had such friends." He called, "Oiving, come here a minute," and a younger man came to his side. "What d'you make of this?"

Irving said, "It ain't African gold. It ain't Indian gold. It ain't a California nugget. I say South America."

"Good boy. Correct."

"How can you tell?" I asked.

He shrugged. "You loin," he said. "How d'you tell the difference between salt and sugar? You loin. . . . The market value of this little bit voigin gold is about forty dollars. I got to make a buck—I'll give you thoity-five."

"Eh?"

"Thoity-six, and not a penny more," he said, counting out the money. "And if your friend gives you any more, come to me with 'em."

I took the money, caught a taxi, and hurried back to MacAroon's place. The bartender was gazing into space.

"That man I was sitting with," I said, "where is he?"

The bartender, with a sardonic smile, said, "He put the bite on you, huh? I can smell a phony a mile off. I didn't like the looks of him as soon as he set foot in my bar. If I was you—"

"Which way did he go?"

"I didn't notice. Soon after you left he ordered a double, no ice and put down a ten-dollar bill—left me fifty cents, and went out."

"Here's my telephone number," I said. "If he turns up again, call me any hour of the day or night, and hold him till I get here. Here's five dollars on account; another five when you call."

But Pilgrim never came to MacAroon's again.

I inquired high and low—mostly low—but found no trace of him. A British-sounding man with an insinuating air, a malarial complexion and a misleading eccentric manner, who talks about the River Amazon and its tributaries —I will pay a substantial reward for information leading to his rediscovery.

The Man with Copper Fingers

DOROTHY L. SAYERS

The Egotists' Club is one of the most genial places in London. It is a place to which you may go when you want to tell that odd dream you had last night, or to announce what a good dentist you have discovered. You can write letters there if you like, and have the temperament of a Jane Austen, for there is no silence room, and it would be a breach of club manners to appear busy or absorbed when another member addresses you. You must not mention golf or fish, however, and, if the Hon. Freddy Arbuthnot's motion is carried at the next committee meeting (and opinion so far appears very favorable), you will not be allowed to mention wireless either. As Lord Peter Wimsey said when the matter was mooted the other day in the smoking-room, those are things you can talk about anywhere. Otherwise the club is not specially exclusive. Nobody is ineligible per se, except strong, silent men. Nominees are, however, required to pass certain tests, whose nature is sufficiently indicated by the fact that a certain distinguished explorer came to grief through accepting, and smoking, a powerful Trichinoply cigar as an accompaniment to a '63 port. On the other hand, dear old Sir Roger Bunt (the coster millionaire who won the £20,000 ballot offered by the *Sunday Shriek,* and used it to found his immense catering business in the Midlands) was highly commended and unanimously elected after declaring frankly that beer and a pipe were all he really cared for in that way. As Lord Peter said again: "Nobody minds coarseness, but one must draw the line at cruelty."

On this particular evening, Masterman (the cubist poet) had brought a guest with him, a man named Varden. Varden had started life as a professional athlete, but a strained heart had obliged him to cut short a brilliant career, and turn his handsome face and remarkably beautiful body to account in the service of the cinema screen. He had come to London from Los Angeles to stimulate publicity for his great new film, *Marathon,* and turned out to be quite a pleasant, unspoiled person—greatly to the relief of the club, since Masterman's guests were apt to be something of a toss-up.

There were only eight men, including Varden, in the brown room that evening. This, with its paneled walls, shaded lamps, and heavy blue curtains was perhaps the cosiest and pleasantest of the small smoking-rooms, of which the club possessed half a dozen or so.

The conversation had begun quite casually by Armstrong's relating a curious little incident which he had witnessed that afternoon at the Temple Station, and Bayes had gone on to say that that was nothing to the really very odd thing which had happened to him, personally, in a thick fog one night in the Euston Road.

Masterman said that the more secluded London squares teemed with subjects for a writer, and instanced his own singular encounter with a weeping woman and a dead monkey, and then Judson took up the tale and narrated how, in a lonely suburb, late at night, he had come upon the dead body of a woman stretched on the pavement with a knife in her side and a policeman standing motionless near by. He had asked if he could do anything, but the policeman had only said, "I wouldn't interfere if I was you, sir; she deserved what she got." Judson said he had not been able to get the incident out of his mind, and then Pettifer told them a queer case in his own medical practice, when a totally unknown man had led him to a house in Bloomsbury where there was a woman suffering from strychnine poisoning. This man had helped him in the most intelligent manner all night, and, when the patient was out of danger, had walked straight out of the house and never reappeared; the odd thing being that, when he (Pettifer) questioned the woman, she answered in great surprise that she had never seen the man in her life and had taken him to be Pettifer's assistant.

"That reminds me," said Varden, "of something still stranger that happened to me once in New York—I've never been able to make out whether it was a madman or a practical joke, or whether I really had a very narrow shave."

This sounded promising, and the guest was urged to go on with his story.

"Well, it really started ages ago," said the actor, "seven years it must have been—just before America came into the war. I was twenty-five at the time, and had been in the film business a little over two years. There was a man called Eric P. Loder, pretty well known in New York at that period, who would have been a very fine sculptor if he hadn't had more money than was good for him, or so I understood from the people who go in for that kind of thing. He used to exhibit a good deal and had a lot of one-man shows of his stuff to which the highbrow people went—he did a good many bronzes, I believe. Perhaps you know about him, Masterman?"

"I've never seen any of his things," said the poet, "but I remember some photographs in *The Art of Tomorrow*. Clever, but rather over-ripe. Didn't he go in for a lot of that chryselephantine stuff? Just to show he could afford to pay for the materials, I suppose."

"Yes, that sounds very like him."

"Of course—and he did a very slick and very ugly realistic group called Lucina, and had the impudence to have it cast in solid gold and stood in his front hall."

"Oh, that thing! Yes—simply beastly I thought it, but then I never could see anything artistic in the idea. Realism, I suppose you'd call it. I like a picture or a statue to make you feel good, or what's it there for? Still, there was something very attractive about Loder."

"How did you come across him?"

"Oh, yes. Well, he saw me in that little picture of mine, *Apollo Comes to New York*—perhaps you remember it. It was my first star part. About a statue that's brought to life—one of the old gods, you know—and how he gets on in a modern city. Dear old Reubenssohn produced it. Now, there was a man who could put a thing through with consummate artistry. You couldn't find an atom of offense from beginning to end, it was all so tasteful, though in the first part one didn't have anything to wear except a sort of scarf—taken from the classical statue, you know."

"The Belvedere?"

"I dare say. Well, Loder wrote me, and said as a sculptor he was interested in me, because I was a good shape and so on, and would I come and pay him a visit in New

York when I was free. So I found out about Loder, and decided it would be good publicity, and when my contract was up, and I had a bit of time to fill in, I went up east and called on him. He was very decent to me, and asked me to stay a few weeks with him while I was looking around.

"He had a magnificent great house about five miles out of the city, crammed full of pictures and antiques and so on. He was somewhere between thirty-five and forty, I should think, dark and smooth, and very quick and lively in his movements. He talked very well, seemed to have been everywhere and have seen everything and not to have any too good an opinion of anybody. You could sit and listen to him for hours; he'd got anecdotes about everybody, from the Pope to old Phineas E. Groot of the Chicago Ring. The only kind of story I didn't care about hearing from him was the improper sort. Not that I don't enjoy an after-dinner story—no, sir, I wouldn't like you to think I was a prig—but he'd tell it with his eyes upon you as if he suspected you of having something to do with it. I've known women do that, and I've seen men do it to women and seen the women squirm, but he was the only man that's ever given me that feeling. Still, apart from that, Loder was the most fascinating fellow I've ever known. And, as I say, his house surely was beautiful, and he kept a first-class table.

"He liked to have everything of the best. There was his mistress, Maria Morano. I don't think I've ever seen anything to touch her, and when you work for the screen you're apt to have a pretty exacting standard of female beauty. She was one of those big, slow, beautifully moving creatures, very placid, with a slow, wide smile. We don't grow them in the States. She'd come from the South—had been a cabaret dancer, he said, and she didn't contradict him. He was very proud of her, and she seemed to be devoted to him in her own fashion. He'd show her off in the studio with nothing on but a fig leaf or so—stand her up beside one of the figures he was always doing of her, and compare them point by point. There was literally only one half inch of her, it seemed, that wasn't absolutely perfect from the sculptor's point of view—the second toe of her left foot was shorter than the big toe. He used to correct it, of course, in the statues. She'd listen to it all with a good-natured smile, sort of vaguely flattered, you know.

Though I think the poor girl sometimes got tired of being gloated over that way. She'd sometimes hunt me out and confide to me that what she had always hoped for was to run a restaurant of her own, with a cabaret show and a great many cooks with white aprons, and lots of polished electric cookers. 'And then I would marry,' she'd say, 'and have four sons and one daughter,' and she told me all the names she had chosen for the family. I thought it was rather pathetic. Loder came in at the end of one of these conversations. He had a sort of a grin on, so I dare say he'd overheard. I don't suppose he attached much importance to it, which shows that he never really understood the girl. I don't think he ever imagined any woman would chuck up the sort of life he'd accustomed her to, and if he was a bit possessive in his manner, at least he never gave her a rival. For all his talk and his ugly statues, she'd got him, and she knew it.

"I stayed there getting on for a month altogether, having a thundering good time. On two occasions Loder had an art spasm, and shut himself up in his studio to work and wouldn't let anybody in for several days on end. He was rather given to that sort of stunt, and when it was over we would have a party, and all Loder's friends and hangers-on would come to have a look at the work of art. He was doing a figure of some nymph or goddess, I fancy, to be cast in silver, and Maria used to go along and sit for him. Apart from those times, he went about everywhere, and we saw all there was to be seen.

"I was fairly annoyed, I admit, when it came to an end. War was declared, and I'd made up my mind to join up when that happened. My heart put me out of the running for trench service, but I counted on getting some sort of a job, with perserverance, so I packed up and went off.

"I wouldn't have believed Loder would have been so genuinely sorry to say good-bye to me. He said over and over again that we'd meet again soon. However, I did get a job with the hospital people, and was sent over to Europe, and it wasn't till 1920 that I saw Loder again.

"He'd written to me before, but I'd had two big pictures to make in '19, and it couldn't be done. However, in '20 I found myself back in New York, doing publicity for *The Passion Streak,* and got a note from Loder begging me to stay with him, and saying he wanted me to sit for him.

Well, that was advertisement that he'd pay for himself, you know, so I agreed. I had accepted an engagement to go out with Mystofilms Ltd. in *Fake of Dead Man's Bush*—the dwarf-men picture, you know, taken on the spot among the Australian bushmen. I wired them that I would join them at Sydney the third week in April, and took my bags out to Loder's.

"Loder greeted me very cordially, though I thought he looked older than when I last saw him. He had certainly grown more nervous in his manner. He was—how shall I describe it?—more intense—more real, in a way. He brought out his pet cynicisms as if he thoroughly meant them, and more and more with that air of getting at you personally. I used to think his disbelief in everything was a kind of artistic pose, but I began to feel I had done him an injustice. He was really unhappy, I could see that quite well, and soon I discovered the reason. As we were driving out in the car I asked for Maria.

" 'She has left me,' he said.

"Well, now, you know, that really surprised me. Honestly, I hadn't thought the girl had that much initiative. 'Why,' I said, 'has she gone and set up in that restaurant of her own she wanted so much?'

" 'Oh! she talked to you about restaurants, did she?' said Loder. 'I suppose you are one of the men that women tell things to. No. She made a fool of herself. She's gone.'

"I didn't quite know what to say. He was so obviously hurt in his vanity, you know, as well as in his feelings. I muttered the usual things, and added that it must be a great loss to his work as well as in other ways. He said it was.

"I asked him when it had happened and whether he'd finished the nymph he was working on before I left. He said, Oh, yes, he'd finished that and done another—something pretty original, which I should like.

"Well, we got to the house and dined, and Loder told me he was going to Europe shortly, a few days after I left myself, in fact. The nymph stood in the dining-room, in a special niche let into the wall. It really was a beautiful thing, not so showy as most of Loder's work, and a wonderful likeness of Maria. Loder put me opposite it, so that I could see it during dinner, and, really, I could hardly take my eyes off it. He seemed very proud of it, and kept on telling me over and over again how glad he was that I liked it. It struck me that he was falling into a trick of repeating himself.

"We went into the smoking-room after dinner. He'd had it rearranged, and the first thing that caught one's eye was a big settee drawn before the fire. It stood about a couple of feet from the ground, and consisted of a base made like a Roman couch, with cushions and a highish back, all made of oak with a silver inlay, and on top of this, forming the actual seat one sat on, if you follow me, there was a great silver figure of a nude woman, fully life-size, lying with her head back and her arms extended along the sides of the couch. A few big loose cushions made it possible to use the thing as an actual settee, though I must say it never was really comfortable to sit on respectably. As a stage prop, for registering dissipation it would have been excellent, but to see Loder sprawling over it by his own fireside gave me a kind of shock. He seemed very much attached to it, though.

" 'I told you,' he said, 'that it was something original.'

"Then I looked more closely at it, and saw that the figure actually was Maria's though the face was rather sketchily done, if you understand what I mean. I suppose he thought a bolder treatment more suited to a piece of furniture.

"But I did begin to think Loder a trifle degenerate when I saw that couch. And in the fortnight that followed I grew more and more uncomfortable with him. That personal manner of his grew more marked every day, and sometimes, while I was giving him sittings, he would sit there and tell one the most beastly things, with his eyes fixed on one in the nastiest way, just to see how one would take it. Upon my word, though he certainly did me uncommonly well, I began to feel I'd be more at ease among the bushmen.

"Well, now I come to the odd thing."

Everybody sat up and listened a little more eagerly.

"It was the evening before I had to leave New York," went on Varden. "I was sitting———"

Here somebody opened the door of the brown room, to be greeted by a warning sign from Bayes. The intruder sank obscurely into a large chair and mixed himself a whisky, with extreme care not to disturb the speaker.

"I was sitting in the smoking-room," continued Varden, "waiting for Loder to come in. I had the house to myself, for Loder had given the servants leave to go to some show or lecture or other, and he himself was getting his things together for his European trip and had had to keep an appointment with this man of business. I must have been very nearly asleep, because it was dusk when I came to with a start and saw a young man quite close to me.

"He wasn't at all like a housebreaker, and still less like a ghost. He was, I might almost say, exceptionally ordinary-looking. He was dressed in a grey English suit, with a fawn overcoat on his arm, and his soft hat and stick in his hand. He had sleek, pale hair, and one of those rather stupid faces, with a long nose and a monocle. I stared at him, for I knew the front door was locked, but before I could get my wits together he spoke. He had a curious, hesitating, husky voice and a strong English accent. He said, surprisingly:

" 'Are you Mr. Varden?'

" 'You have the advantage of me,' I said.

"He said, 'Please excuse my butting in; I know it looks like bad manners, but you'd better clear out of this place very quickly, don't you know.'

" 'What the hell do you mean?' I said.

"He said, 'I don't mean it in any impertinent way, but you must realize that Loder's never forgiven you, and I'm afraid he means to make you into a hatstand or an electric-light fitting, or something of that sort.'

"My God! I can tell you I felt queer. It was such a quiet voice, and his manners were perfect, and yet the words were quite meaningless! I remembered that madmen are supposed to be extra strong, and edged toward the bell—and then it came over me with rather a chill that I was alone in the house.

" 'How did you get here?' I asked, putting a bold face on it.

" 'I'm afraid I picked the lock,' he said, as casually as though he were apologizing for not having a card about him. 'I couldn't be sure Loder hadn't come back. But I do really think you had better get out as quickly as possible.'

" 'See here,' I said, 'who are you and what the hell are you driving at? What do you mean about Loder never forgiving me? Forgiving me what?'

" 'Why,' he said, 'about—you will pardon me prancing in on your private affairs, won't you—about Maria Morano.'

" 'What about her, in the devil's name?' I cried. 'What do you know about her, anyway? She went off while I was at the war. What's it to do with me?'

" 'Oh!' said the very odd young man. 'I beg your pardon. Perhaps I have been relying too much on Loder's judgment. Damned foolish; but the possibility of his being mistaken did not occur to me. He fancies you were Maria Morano's lover when you were here last time.'

" 'Maria's lover?' I said. 'Preposterous! She went off with her man, whoever he was. He must know she didn't go with me.'

" 'Maria never left the house,' said the young man, 'and if you don't get out of it this moment, I won't answer for your ever leaving, either.'

" 'In God's name,' I cried, exasperated, 'what do you mean?'

"The man turned and threw the blue cushions off the foot of the silver couch.

" 'Have you ever examined the toes of this?' he asked.

" 'Not particularly,' I said, more and more astonished. 'Why should I?'

" 'Did you ever know Loder to make any figure of her but this with that short toe on the left foot?' he went on.

"Well, I did take a look at it then, and saw it was as he said—the left foot had a short second toe.

" 'So it is,' I said, 'but, after all, why not?'

" 'Why not, indeed?' said the young man. 'Wouldn't you like to see why, of all the figures Loder made of Maria Morano, this is the only one that has the feet of the living woman?'

"He picked up the poker.

" 'Look!' he said.

"With a lot more strength than I should have expected from him, he brought the head of the poker down with a heavy crack on the silver couch. It struck one of the arms of the figure neatly at the elbow-joint, smashing a jagged hole in the silver. He wrenched at the arm and brought it away. It was hollow, and, as I am alive, I tell you there was a long, dry arm-bone inside it!"

Varden paused, and put away a good mouthful of whisky.

"Well?" cried several breathless voices.

"Well," said Varden, "I'm not ashamed to say I went out of that house like an old buck-rabbit that hears the man with the gun. There was a car standing just outside, and the driver opened the door. I tumbled in, and then it came over me that the whole thing might be a trap, and I tumbled out again and ran till I reached the trolley-cars. But I found my bags at the station next day, duly registered for Vancouver.

"When I pulled myself together I did rather wonder what Loder was thinking about my disappearance, but I could no more have gone back into that horrible house than I could have taken poison. I left for Vancouver next morning, and from that day to this I never saw either of those men again. I've still not the faintest idea who the fair man was, or what became of him, but I heard in a roundabout way that Loder was dead—in some kind of an accident, I fancy."

There was a pause. Then:

"It's a damned good story, Mr. Varden," said Armstrong —he was a dabbler in various kinds of handiwork, and was, indeed, chiefly responsible for Mr. Arbuthnot's motion to ban wireless—"but are you suggesting there was a complete skeleton inside that silver casting? Do you mean Loder put it into the core of the mold when the casting was done? It would be awfully difficult and dangerous—the slightest accident would have put him at the mercy of his workmen. And that statue must have been considerably over life-size to allow of the skeleton being well covered."

"Mr. Varden has unintentionally misled you, Armstrong," said a quiet, husky voice suddenly from the shadow behind Varden's chair. "The figure was not silver, but electro-plated on a copper base deposited direct on the body. The lady was Sheffield-plated, in fact. I fancy the soft parts of her must have been digested away with pepsin, or some preparation of the kind, after the process was complete, but I can't be positive about that."

"Hullo, Wimsey," said Armstrong, "was that you came in just now? And why this confident pronouncement?"

The effect of Wimsey's voice on Varden had been extraordinary. He had leapt to his feet, and turned the lamp so as to light up Wimsey's face.

"Good evening, Mr. Varden," said Lord Peter. "I'm delighted to meet you again and to apologize for my unceremonious behavior on the occasion of our last encounter."

Varden took the proffered hand, but was speechless.

"D'you mean to say, you mad mystery-monger, that you were Varden's Great Unknown?" demanded Bayes. "Ah, well," he added rudely, "we might have guessed it from his vivid description."

"Well, since you're here," said Smith-Hartington, the Morning Yell man, "I think you ought to come across with the rest of the story."

"Was it just a joke?" asked Judson.

"Of course not," interrupted Pettifer, before Lord Peter had time to reply. "Why should it be? Wimsey's seen enough queer things not to have to waste his time inventing them."

"That's true enough," said Bayes. "Comes of having deductive powers and all that sort of thing, and always sticking one's nose into things that are better not investigated."

"That's all very well, Bayes," said his lordship, "but if I hadn't just mentioned the matter to Mr. Varden that evening, where would he be?"

"Ah, where? That's exactly what we want to know," demanded Smith-Hartington. "Come on, Wimsey, no shirking; we must have the tale."

"And the whole tale," added Pettifer.

"And nothing but the tale," said Armstrong, dexterously whisking away the whisky-bottle and the cigars from under Lord Peter's nose. "Get on with it, old son. Not a smoke do you smoke and not a sup do you sip till Burd Ellen is set free."

"Brute!" said his lordship plaintively. "As a matter of fact," he went on, with a change of tone, "it's not really a story I want to get about. It might land me in a very unpleasant sort of position—manslaughter, probably, and murder possibly."

"Gosh!" said Bayes.

"That's all right," said Armstrong, "nobody's going to talk. We can't afford to lose you from the club, you know. Smith-Hartington will have to control his passion for copy, that's all."

Pledges of discretion having been given all around, Lord Peter settled himself back and began his tale.

"The curious case of Eric P. Loder affords one more instance of the strange manner in which some power beyond our puny human wills arranges the affairs of men. Call it Providence—call it Destiny———"

"We'll call it off," said Bayes, "you can leave out that part."

Lord Peter groaned and began again.

"Well, the first thing that made me feel a bit inquisitive about Loder was a casual remark by a man at the Emigration Office in New York, where I happened to go about that silly affair of Mrs. Bilt's. He said, 'What on earth is Eric Loder going to do in Australia? I should have thought Europe was more in his line.'

" 'Australia?' I said, 'you're wandering, dear old thing. He told me the other day he was off to Italy in three weeks' time.'

" 'Italy, nothing,' he said, 'he was all over our place today, asking about how you got to Sydney and what were the necessary formalities, and so on.'

" 'Oh,' I said, 'I suppose he's going by the Pacific route, and calling at Sydney on his way.' But I wondered why he hadn't said so when I'd met him the day before. He had distinctly talked about sailing for Europe and doing Paris before he went on to Rome.

"I felt so darned inquisitive that I went and called on Loder two nights later.

"He seemed quite pleased to see me, and was full of his forthcoming trip. I asked him again about his route, and he told me quite distinctly he was going via Paris.

"Well, that was that, and it wasn't really any of my business, and we chatted about other things. He told me that Mr. Varden was coming to stay with him before he went, and that he hoped to get him to pose for a figure before he left. He said he'd never seen a man so perfectly formed. 'I meant to get him to do it before,' he said, 'but war broke out, and he went and joined the army before I had time to start.'

"He was lolling on that beastly couch of his at the time, and, happening to look round at him, I caught such a nasty sort of glitter in his eye that it gave me quite a turn. He was stroking the figure over the neck and grinning at it.

" 'None of your efforts in Sheffield plate, I hope,' said I.

" 'Well,' he said, 'I thought of making a kind of companion to this, The Sleeping Athlete, you know, or something of that sort.'

" 'You'd much better cast it,' I said. 'Why did you put the stuff on so thick? It destroys the fine detail.'

"That annoyed him. He never liked to hear any objection made to that work of art.

" 'This was experimental,' he said. 'I mean the next to be a real masterpiece. You'll see.'

"We'd got to about that point when the butler came in to ask should he make up a bed for me, as it was such a bad night. We hadn't noticed the weather particularly, though it had looked a bit threatening when I started from New York. However, we now looked out, and saw that it was coming down in sheets and torrents. It wouldn't have mattered, only that I'd only brought a little open racing car and no overcoat, and certainly the prospect of five miles in that downpour wasn't altogether attractive. Loder urged me to stay, and I said I would.

"I was feeling a bit fagged, so I went to bed right off. Loder said he wanted to do a bit of work in the studio first, and I saw him depart along the corridor.

"You won't allow me to mention Providence, so I'll only say it was a very remarkable thing that I should have woken up at two in the morning to find myself lying in a pool of water. The man had stuck a hot-water bottle into the bed, because it hadn't been used just lately, and the beastly thing had gone and unstoppered itself. I lay awake for ten minutes in the deeps of damp misery before I had sufficient strength of mind to investigate. Then I found it was hopeless—sheets, blankets, mattress, all soaked. I looked at the arm-chair, and then I had a brilliant idea. I remembered there was a lovely great divan in the studio, with a big skin rug and a pile of cushions. Why not finish the night there? I took the little electric torch which always goes about with me, and started off.

"The studio was empty, so I supposed Loder had finished and trotted off to roost. The divan was there, all right, with a screen drawn partly across it, so I rolled myself up under the rug and prepared to snooze off.

"I was just getting beautifully sleepy again when I heard footsteps, not in the passage, but apparently on the other side of the room. I was surprised, because I didn't know there was any way out in that direction. I lay low, and presently I saw a streak of light appear from the cupboard where Loder kept his tools and things. The streak widened, and Loder emerged, carrying an electric torch. He closed the cupboard door very gently after him, and padded across the studio. He stopped before the easel and uncovered it; I could see him through a crack in the screen. He stood for some minutes gazing at a sketch on the easel, and then gave one of the nastiest gurgly laughs I've ever had the pleasure of hearing. If I'd ever seriously thought of announcing my unauthorized presence I abandoned all idea of it then. Presently he covered the easel again, and went out by the door at which I had come in.

"I waited till I was sure he had gone, and then got up—uncommonly quietly, I may say. I tiptoed over to the easel to see what the fascinating work of art was. I saw at once it was the design for the figure of The Sleeping Athlete, and as I looked at it I felt a sort of horrid conviction stealing over me. It was an idea which seemed to begin in my stomach, and work its way up to the roots of my hair.

"My family says I'm too inquisitive. I can only say that wild horses wouldn't have kept me from investigating that cupboard. With the feeling that something absolutely vile might hop out at me—I was a bit wrought up, and it was a rotten time of night—I put a heroic hand on the door knob.

"To my astonishment, the thing wasn't even locked. It opened at once, to show a range of perfectly innocent and orderly shelves, which wouldn't possibly have held Loder.

"My blood was up, you know, by this time, so I hunted round for the spring-lock which I knew must exist, and found it without much difficulty. The back of the cupboard swung noiselessly inwards, and I found myself at the top of a narrow flight of stairs.

"I had the sense to stop and see that the door could be opened from the inside before I went any farther, and I also selected a good stout pestle which I found on the shelves as a weapon in case of accident. Then I closed the door and tripped with elflike lightness down that jolly old staircase.

"There was another door at the bottom, but it didn't take me long to fathom the secret of that. Feeling frightfully excited, I threw it boldly open, with the pestle ready for action.

"However, the room seemed to be empty. My torch caught the gleam of something liquid, and then I found the wall-switch.

"I saw a biggish square room, fitted up as a workshop. On the right-hand wall was a big switchboard, with a bench beneath it. From the middle of the ceiling hung a great floodlight, illuminating a glass vat, fully seven feet long by about three wide. I turned on the floodlight, and looked down into the vat. It was filled with a dark brown liquid which I recognized as the usual compound of cyanide and copper sulphate which they use for copper-plating.

"The rods hung over it with their hooks all empty, but there was a packing-case half-opened at one side of the room, and, pulling the covering aside, I could see rows of copper anodes—enough of them to put a plating over a quarter of an inch thick on a life-size figure. There was a smaller case, still nailed up, which from its weight and appearance I guessed to contain the silver for the rest of the process. There was something else I was looking for, and I soon found it—considerable quantity of prepared graphite and a big jar of varnish.

"Of course, there was no evidence, really, of anything being on the cross. There was no reason why Loder shouldn't make a plaster cast and Sheffield-plate it if he had a fancy for that kind of thing. But then I found something that couldn't have come there legitimately.

"On the bench was an oval slab of copper about an inch and a half long—Loder's night's work, I guessed. It was an electrotype of the American Consular seal, the thing they stamp on your passport photograph to keep you from hiking it off and substituting the picture of your friend Mr. Jiggs, who would like to get out of the country because he is so popular with Scotland Yard.

"I sat down on Loder's stool, and worked out that pretty little plot in all its details. I could see it all turned on three things. First of all, I must find out if Varden was proposing to make tracks shortly for Australia, because, if he wasn't, it threw all my beautiful theories out. And, secondly, it would help matters greatly if he happened to have dark hair like Loder's, as he has, you see—near enough, anyway, to fit the description on a passport. I'd only seen him in that Apollo Belvedere thing, with a fair wig on. But I knew if I hung about I should see him presently when he came to stay with Loder. And, thirdly, of course, I had to discover if Loder was likely to have any grounds for a grudge against Varden.

"Well, I figured out I'd stayed down in that room about as long as was healthy. Loder might come back at any moment, and I didn't forget that a vatful of copper sulphate and cyanide of potassium would be a highly handy means of getting rid of a too-inquisitive guest. And I can't say I had any great fancy for figuring as part of Loder's domestic furniture. I've always hated things made in the shape of things—volumes of Dickens that turn out to be a biscuit-tin, and dodges like that; and, though I take no overwhelming interest in my own funeral, I should like it to be in good taste. I went so far as to wipe away any finger-marks I might have left behind me, and then I went back to the studio and rearranged that divan. I didn't feel Loder would care to think I'd been down there.

"There was just one other thing I felt inquisitive about. I tiptoed back through the hall and into the smoking-room. The silver couch glimmered in the light of the torch. I felt I disliked it fifty times more than ever before. However, I pulled myself together and took a careful look at the feet of the figure. I'd heard all about that second toe of Maria Morano's.

"I passed the rest of the night in the arm-chair after all.

"What with Mrs. Bilt's job and one thing and another, and the enquiries I had to make, I had to put off my interference in Loder's little game till rather late. I found out that Varden had been staying with Loder a few months before the beautiful Maria Morano had vanished. I'm afraid I was rather stupid about that, Mr. Varden. I thought perhaps there had been something."

"Don't apologize," said Varden, with a little laugh. "Cinema actors are notoriously immoral."

"Why rub it in?" said Wimsey, a trifle hurt. "I apologize. Anyway, it came to the same thing as far as Loder was concerned. Then there was one bit of evidence I had to get to be absolutely certain. Electro-plating—especially such a ticklish job as the one I had in mind—wasn't a job that could be finished in a night; on the other hand, it seemed necessary that Mr. Varden should be seen alive in New York up to the day he was scheduled to depart. It was also clear that Loder meant to be able to prove that a Mr. Varden had left New York all right, according to plan, and had actually arrived in Sydney. Accordingly, a false Mr. Varden was to depart with Varden's papers and Varden's passport furnished with a new photograph duly stamped with the Consular stamp, and to disappear quietly at Sydney and be retransformed into Mr. Eric Loder, traveling with a perfectly regular passport of his own. Well, then, in that case, obviously a cablegram would have to be sent off to Mystofilms Ltd., warning them to expect Varden by a later boat than he had arranged. I handed over this part of the job to my man, Bunter, who is uncommonly capable. The devoted fellow shadowed Loder faithfully for getting on for three weeks, and at length, the very day before Mr. Varden was due to depart, the cablegram was sent from an office in Broadway, where, by a happy Providence (once more) they supply extremely hard pencils."

"By Jove!" cried Varden, "I remember now being told something about a cablegram when I got out, but I never connected it with Loder. I thought it was just some stupidity of the telegraph people."

"Quite so. Well, as soon as I'd got that, I popped along to Loder's with a picklock in one pocket and an automatic in the other. The good Bunter went with me, and, if I didn't return by a certain time, had orders to telephone for the police. So you see everything was pretty well covered. Bunter was the chauffeur who was waiting for you, Mr. Varden, but you turned suspicious—I don't blame you altogether—so all we could do was forward your luggage along to the train.

"On the way out we met the Loder servants en route for New York in a car, which showed us that we were on the right track, and also that I was going to have a fairly simple job of it.

"You've heard all about my interview with Mr. Varden. I really don't think I could improve upon his account. When I'd seen him and his traps safely off the premises, I made for the studio. It was empty, so I opened the secret door, and, as I expected, saw a line of light under the workshop door at the far end of the passage."

"So Loder was there all the time?"

"Of course he was. I took my little pop-gun tight in my fist and opened the door very gently. Loder was standing between the tank and the switchboard, very busy indeed—so busy he didn't hear me come in. His hands were black with graphite, a big heap of which was spread on a sheet on the floor, and he was engaged with a long, springy coil of copper wire, running to the output of the transformer. The big packing-case had been opened, and all the hooks were occupied.

" 'Loder!' I said.

"He turned on me with a face like nothing human. 'Wimsey!' he shouted. 'What the hell are you doing here?'

" 'I have come,' I said, 'to tell you that I know how the apple gets into the dumpling.' And I showed him the automatic.

"He gave a great yell and dashed at the switchboard, turning out the light, so that I could not see to aim. I heard him leap at me—and then there came in the darkness a crash and a splash—and a shriek such as I never heard—not in five years of war—and never want to hear again.

"I groped forward for the switchboard. Of course, I turned on everything before I could lay my hand on the light, but I got it at last—a great white glare from the floodlight over the vat.

"He lay there, still twitching faintly. Cyanide, you see, is about the swiftest and painfulest thing out. Before I could move to do anything, I knew he was dead—poisoned and drowned and dead. The coil of wire that had tripped him had gone into the vat with him. Without thinking, I touched it, and got a shock that pretty well staggered me. Then I realized that I must have turned on the current when I was hunting for the light. I looked into the vat again. As he fell, his hands had clutched at the wire. The coils were tight around his fingers, and the current was methodically depositing a film of copper all over his hands, which were blackened with the graphite.

"I had just sense enough to realize that Loder was dead, and that it might be a nasty sort of look-out for me if the thing came out, for I'd certainly gone along to threaten him with a pistol.

"I searched about till I found some solder and an iron. Then I went upstairs and called in Bunter, who had done his ten miles in record time. We went into the smoking-room and soldered the arm of that cursed figure into place again, as well as we could, and then we took everything back into the workshop. We cleaned off every fingerprint and removed every trace of our presence. We left the light and the switchboard as they were, and returned to New York by an extremely roundabout route. The only thing we brought away with us was the facsimile of the Consular seal, and that we threw into the river.

"Loder was found by the butler next morning. We read in the papers how he had fallen into the vat when engaged on some experiments in electro-plating. The ghastly fact was commented upon that the dead man's hands were thickly coppered over. They couldn't get it off without irreverent violence, so he was buried like that.

"That's all. Please, may I have my whisky-and-soda now?"

"What happened to the couch?" enquired Smith-Hartington.

"I bought it at the sale of Loder's things." said Wimsey, "and got hold of a dear old Catholic priest I knew, to whom I told the whole story under strict vow of secrecy. He was a very sensible and feeling old bird; so one moonlight night Bunter and I carried the thing out in the car to his own little church, some miles out of the city, and gave it Christian burial in a corner of the graveyard. It seemed the best thing to do."

Levitation

JOSEPH PAYNE BRENNAN

Morgan's Wonder Carnival moved into Riverville for an overnight stand, setting up its tents in the big ball park on the edge of the village. It was a warm evening in early October and by seven o'clock a sizable crowd had made its way to the scene of raucous amusement.

The traveling show was neither large nor particularly impressive of its type, but its appearance was eagerly welcomed in Riverville, an isolated mountain community many miles from the motion picture houses, vaudeville theatres and sports arenas situated in larger towns.

The natives of Riverville did not demand sophisticated entertainment; consequently the inevitable Fat Lady, the Tattooed Man and the Monkey Boy kept them chattering animatedly for many minutes at a time. They crammed peanuts and buttered popcorn into their mouths, drank cup after cup of pink lemonade, and got their fingers all but stuck together trying to scrape the paper wrappers off colored taffy candies.

Everyone appeared to be in a relaxed and tolerant state of mind when the barker for the Hypnotist began his spiel. The barker, a short stocky man wearing a checkered suit, bellowed through an improvised megaphone, while the Hypnotist himself remained aloof at the rear of the plank platform erected in front of his tent. He appeared disinterested, scornful, and he scarcely deigned to glance at the gathering crowd.

At length, however, when some fifty souls had assembled in front of the platform, he stepped forward into the light. A murmur went up from the crowd.

In the harsh overhead electric glare, the Hypnotist made a striking appearance. His tall figure, thin to the point of emaciation, his pale complexion, and most of all his dark, sunken eyes, enormous and brilliant, compelled immediate attention. His dress, a severe black suit and an archaic black string tie, added a final Mephistophelean touch.

He surveyed the crowd coolly, with an expression betraying resignation and a kind of quiet contempt.

His sonorous voice reached to the far edge of the throng. "I will require one volunteer from among you," he said. "If someone will kindly step up—"

Everyone glanced around, or nudged his neighbor, but nobody advanced toward the platform.

The Hypnotist shrugged. "There can be no demonstration," he said in a weary voice, "unless one of you is kind enough to come up. I assure you, ladies and gentlemen, the demonstration is quite harmless, quite without danger."

He looked around expectantly and presently a young man slowly elbowed through the crowd toward the platform.

The Hypnotist helped him up the steps and seated him in a chair.

"Relax," said the Hypnotist. "Presently you will be asleep and you will do exactly what I tell you to do."

The young man squirmed on the chair, grinning self-consciously toward the crowd.

The Hypnotist caught his attention, fixing his enormous eyes on him, and the young man stopped squirming.

Suddenly someone in the crowd threw a large ball of colored popcorn toward the platform. The popcorn arched over the lights, landing squarely atop the head of the young man sitting in the chair.

He jerked sideways, almost falling off the chair, and the crowd, quiet a moment before, guffawed boisterously.

The Hypnotist was furious. He turned scarlet and literally shook with rage as he glared at the crowd.

"Who threw that?" he demanded in a choking voice.

The crowd grew silent.

The Hypnotist continued to glare at them. At length the color left his face and he stopped trembling, but his brilliant eyes remained baleful.

Finally he nodded to the young man seated on the platform, dismissing him with brief thanks, and turned again toward the crowd.

"Due to the interruption," he announced in a low voice,

"it will be necessary to recommence the demonstration—with a new subject. Perhaps the person who threw the popcorn would care to come up?"

At least a dozen people in the crowd turned to gaze at someone who stood half in shadow at the rear of the gathering.

The Hypnotist spotted him at once; his dark eyes seemed to smoulder. "Perhaps," he said in a purring, mocking voice, "the one who interrupted is afraid to come up. He prefers to hide in the shadows and throw popcorn!"

The culprit voiced a sudden exclamation and then pushed belligerently toward the platform. His appearance was not in any way remarkable; in fact, he somewhat resembled the first young man, and any casual observer would have placed the two of them in the farm-laborer class, neither more nor less capable than the average.

The second young man sat down in the platform chair with a distinct air of defiance and for some minutes visibly fought the Hypnotist's suggestion to relax. Presently, however, his aggressiveness disappeared and he dutifully stared into the smouldering eyes opposite his own.

In another minute or two he arose at the Hypnotist's command and lay flat on his back on the hard planks of the platform. The crowd gasped.

"You will fall asleep," the Hypnotist told him. "You will fall asleep. You are falling asleep. You are falling asleep. You are asleep and you will do anything which I command you to do. Anything which I command you to do. Anything. . . ."

His voice droned on, repeating repetitious phrases, and the crowd grew perfectly silent.

Suddenly a new note entered the Hypnotist's voice and the audience became tense.

"Do not stand up—but *rise from the platform!*" the Hypnotist commanded. *"Rise from the platform!"* His dark eyes became wild and luminous-looking and the crowd shivered.

"Rise!"

Then the crowd drew in its collective breath with an audible start.

The young man lying rigid on the platform, without moving a muscle, began to ascend horizontally. He arose slowly, almost imperceptively at first, but soon with a steady and unmistakable acceleration.

"Rise!" the Hypnotist's voice rang out.

The young man continued to ascend, until he was feet off the platform, and still he did not stop.

The crowd was sure it was some kind of trick, but in spite of themselves they stared open-mouthed. The young man appeared to be suspended and moving in mid-air without any possible means of physical support.

Abruptly the focus of the crowd's attention was shifted; the Hypnotist clasped a hand to his chest, staggered, and crumpled to the platform.

There were calls for a doctor. The barker in the checkered suit appeared out of the tent and bent over the motionless form.

He felt for a pulse, shook his head and straightened up. Someone offered a bottle of whiskey, but he merely shrugged.

Suddenly a woman in the crowd screamed.

Everyone turned to look at her and a second later followed the direction of her gaze.

Immediately there were further cries—for the young man whom the Hypnotist had put to sleep was still ascending. While the crowd's attention had been distracted by the fatal collapse of the Hypnotist, he had continued to rise. He was now a good seven feet above the platform and moving inexorably upward. Even after the death of the Hypnotist, he continued to obey that final ringing command: *"Rise!"*

The barker, eyes all but popping out of his head, made a frantic upward leap, but he was too short. His fingers barely brushed the moving figure above and he fell heavily back to the platform.

The rigid form of the young man continued to float upward, as if he were being hoisted by some kind of invisible pulley.

Women began screaming hysterically; men shouted. But no one knew what to do. A look of terror crept over the face of the barker as he stared up. Once he glanced wildly toward the sprawled shape of the Hypnotist.

"Come down, Frank! Come down!" the crowd shrieked. "Frank! Wake up! Come down! Stop! Frank!"

But the rigid form of Frank moved ever upward. Up,

up, until he was level with the top of the carnival tent, until he reached the height of the tallest trees—until he passed the trees and moved on into the soft moonlit sky of early October.

Many in the crowd threw hands over horror-stricken faces and turned away.

Those who continued to stare saw the floating form ascend into the sky until it was no more than a tiny speck, like a little cinder drifting far up near the moon.

Then it disappeared altogether.

Miss Winters and the Wind

CHRISTINE NOBLE GOVAN

Miss Winters stood on the corner with her bus transfer held tightly in her hand and hated the wind. There had been a feud between Miss Winters and the wind for all the years that she had lived in this flat, dreadful city. It seemed to pick her out—a lone, forlorn little figure—to vent its nasty, playful vindictiveness upon. It pulled at her droopy felt hat and whipped her straggly hair about her face, grabbed up her skirt in bawdy mischief, exposing her black cotton stockings.

Once, when she had been coming home from her work, it had snatched the transfer from her hand and blown it under a passing bus. When the bus had gone, Miss Winters had peered through the dusk, searching everywhere; but the bit of yellow paper eluded her. People crowding about her had almost pushed her under a truck and had sworn at her impatiently. It had been the day before payday and she had only the fare back to work in the morning. She had to walk the rest of the way home—three miles, and all against the wind.

When she had lived in the South as a child, the wind had been a lovesome thing. The mountains kept it properly in hand and broke it as one breaks a mettlesome colt. It blew against the mountain tops and was parted into bits by the trees, which roiled and hummed with a sound like the sea. Over the fields, wild broom swept gently, making them rippling, molten seas of red-gold, liquid beauty. In school, when she read *Hiawatha,* her narrow face lighted momentarily at the lines:

> As in sunshine gleam the ripples
> That the cold wind makes in rivers.

She had not known what a cold wind really was.

But now she knew. It was what seeped in at the ledges and made her feet numb in spite of the fire she so assiduously tended. It got into bed with her at night so that even her striped cat which crept under the covers shivered, getting up all through the cold black hours to turn his aching bones and seek to warm another surface. It blew through her worn coat and crept into the jagged hole in her flannel bloomers, where she had snagged them on the wire clothesline on the roof. It tore at her fingers in their patched gloves until they burned in an agony of freezing.

Her mother had come from this unspeakable section. And after Miss Winters' father had died, the old lady had yearned to come home. The wind had been too much for her, Miss Winters remembered with grim satisfaction. Two seasons of it and the old lady had been carried off with pleurisy.

Miss Winters had had a fairly comfortable business then. She did "Fine and Fancy Sewing, Prices Reasonable." A flat-chested spinster, whose maidenly longings had burned to a black ash years before, she made babies' frocks with minute embroidered yokes as delicate as frost, bridal gowns, and perky pinafores for chubby little girls.

Her mother's illness and death was an expense. The depression came. She moved to meaner quarters, quarters evidently coveted by the wind, since it came in at every opportunity. She was lonely and anxious and sometimes afraid. Fear clutched at her throat like an actual hand, making it difficult to swallow.

Then the WPA gave her sewing to do. She made thick sacks and heavy work garments. Her hands grew stiff and raw at the clumsy work, and she thought of the women she had draped in silk and crepe de Chine, of the flounced embroideries of her girlhood.

The worst blow came when the project was closed. Women wore slacks and worked in factories and bought ready-made things. They had no time to try on Miss Winters' meticulously fashioned garments. Her old customers died or went to Florida where the wind was less bitter. Miss Winters' fright crept over her like a slowly rising tide. The hands which had once fashioned sprays of lilies of the valley on batiste and lawn had grown arthritic with the cold and with coarse work. All she could get was mending now, and occasional work at an alteration shop.

The bus was crowded, and Miss Winters had to stand. On the street in which she lived, the cold had killed even the smell of garlic and cabbage. But the wind was there blowing the papers about, sending smoke and dust into her face and tugging at her hat until her eyes filled with tears of vexation.

She had two flights of stairs to climb before she got to her rooms. The cat was there waiting, curled up in the middle of the bed. He jumped down, stretching his lanky, striped body, and called to her—the only creature left who greeted her as a friend. With the cat she could sometimes forget the clutching fear. His confidence in her gave her a meager courage and determination. Yet she feared for him, too; so many people were unkind to cats, especially if they were homeless.

"Wuzee lonesome, muzzer's boofu puwussycat?" she asked through chapped lips. "Muzzer'll build ums a fire. Muzzer'll feed him."

The cat, as if in appreciation of such obviously idiotic devotion, writhed against her skirt and purred.

Miss Winters, still gloved, laid the sticks and the precious bits of coal in the ashy grate and set a match to them. The damned wind came down the chimney and blew out the flame, scattering ashes over the hearth and over her desperately polished shoes.

At last she got the fire burning feebly. She set a pan of water on the gas ring for tea. While it heated, she sat in the deep-bottomed rocker before the hearth, her legs spread comfortably, her hands folded against her body for warmth. The cat jumped on her lap, nudging her with determined, silken buttings under the chin, and she put her arms around him gratefully. He was something alive in the bare room, something to make her forget a little the rising tide of her fright. The rent—it took all she made at the shop—there was the thirty-seven cents due the milkman—her shoe soles—the fear was always there. Haunted by it, she had bungled a garment at the alteration shop and had nearly lost her day's work there. Cold that was not from the wind filled her at the memory.

The cat stood on his legs, purring and sliding his velvety nose against her face, making a winning sound that was both a purr and a mew. In a sudden burst of tenderness she hugged him to her and he stared up at her smugly, his eyes green moons with mysteriously golden crevices in them.

She jumped up and made the tea, pouring a little milk from a can and some of the hot water into a saucer for the cat. From her purse she took a chop bone she had wheedled from one of her fellow workers. It had a sliver of meat upon it and gave forth an enticing fragrance of pepper and fried flesh. She pulled the meat off, looking about the bare room shamefacedly, and ate it slowly, tears of self-pity welling for a moment in her eyes. Then she stooped and set the bone with its ruffle of cold suet by the cat's saucer. The cat left the milk and began to gnaw fastidiously at the suet, the tip of his tail curling in and out with satisfaction.

Miss Winters took off her hat and drank her tea. She sat and sipped it and watched the cat, savoring the beauty of his gaunt grace and the wonder of his green and depthless eyes.

The wind was rising. The room grew colder and colder as the darkness deepened. Miss Winters took off her outer garments and brought her flannel gown and heated it by the fire. She heated more water and filled a fruit jar to slip between the frigid sheets. Then, armed with the cat and the jar, and banking the meager coals to hold the heat as long as possible, she crept into bed. The spotted bulb beside her bed gave scarcely enough light to read the sensational love-story magazine with which she escaped into forgetfulness each night.

Hours later she was awakened. The wind, not content to torment her by day, to make every waking hour a misery and a threat, must arouse her by night and bring her back to the grim knowledge from which in her dreams she had a brief escape.

It howled around the chimney, it battered the windows so that they rattled in their frames. The window that Miss Winters had patched with a wide piece of butcher's paper seemed to bulge as if at any moment it would burst and hurtle across the room.

Something blew down on the roof and continued to rattle and bounce, making it impossible to sleep. The cold seemed a tangible thing, raking her spine, nipping her face, pinching at her feet where the already chilly fruit jar mocked any idea of comfort. She turned on the light as

though it might warm her. The cat crawled out and
nervously about the bed.

There came a particularly vicious gust of wind. It screamed and threw itself at the cracked window. The glass ripped apart and was scattered like shrapnel. The cat leaped from the bed, meeting a spear of the glass in midair. He gave a scream and dropped wearily. Over the yellowish matting rug the bright splashes of his blood were blown like the petals of a rose.

Miss Winters rose from the intricate wrappings of the bed. She was cold, but with the cold of insensate fury. She went across the broken glass and picked up the limp body. The lovely green eyes were glazing and the blood dripped in warm splotches on her stockinged feet.

She stood there for a long, long time. At last she laid the cat down and said absently, "This has gone far enough."

She knew at last what she must do, and consequently felt calm. Going to the bed, she ripped off the covers, the coat she wore in the daytime, the quilt that was made of all the velvet and silks of her happier days. She got the sheet, a huge, patched affair, and she shook it out, looking at it thoughtfully.

It was so clear, so simple, that she wondered she had not thought of it before. She must catch the wind and tie it firmly in something so that never again could it get away, frightening and harassing poor old women, keeping them awake to the knowledge of their misery, killing their cats. She put on her shoes and, without giving the cat another look, opened the door and began to walk resolutely down the stairs.

"Who has seen the wind?" she sang in the treble of her childhood, as the wind tore at her long flannel gown and tried to take the sheet away from her.

"Ha! Ha!" she chuckled, holding the sheet closer to her. "Not this time, my fine friend! Not this time!"

"Who has seen the wind? Where does the wind go—up high—up high, high in the sky!"

She looked at the church steeple. It was the highest thing in sight. It shone there even on this dark night, a dull, gleaming spear. A spear had killed the cat. The wind had a spear. She would kill the wind.

"Q.E.D.," she chuckled, from some forgotten pigeon-hole.

You got at the tower of the church through a little door in the rear. As she had expected, it was not locked, and without hesitation she began her purposeful ascent. Up and up, around and around, tripping over the sheet, stepping on the hem of her gown, stumbling, laughing and going on again. There was no wind inside the tower, but she was not deceived. It was waiting for her at the top—*and she was waiting for it!*

At last she reached the little room where the chimes were, a square room with open Gothic arches and a balcony off to one side. The wind was there, as she expected, ramping and growling about like a lion. But she was no longer afraid of it.

"We shall see!" she crooned happily. "We shall see!"

She shook out the sheet. Of course the wind tried to take it, but she caught the four corners together skillfully and stepped out on the little ledge. The lights in the town glimmered and twinkled far below. She looked at them placidly as if to say, "Just watch me! I'm fixing this devilish fellow once and for all!"

Just then the wind came at her. It gave a swoop and she caught it in the sheet which billowed like a huge loaf of rising bread. She had to leap to get it, but she had it there! She was so happy, so relieved, she felt as though she were simply walking on air!

She looked down and the lights rushed toward her. She had one icy moment before she died—one moment in which to know that the wind had won.

The Dog Died First

BRUNO FISCHER

Blood was on my mind that night, but it was blood of the French Revolution. I was correcting Modern European History papers while Dot was at a hen party at Marie Cannon's. At midnight I went to bed, knowing that between bridge and chitchat there was no telling when Dot would be home.

The sound of the car pulling into the driveway woke me. As we have no garage in our bungalow-type stucco house, we leave the car out in the open on the cinder driveway. I heard Dot enter the house through the back door, and then I was listening to water running in the kitchen.

It ran for a long time—too long for her to be getting a drink and she certainly wouldn't be washing herself at the kitchen sink. Drowsily I was wondering what she was up to now, and I wondered a lot more when she turned off the water and left the house again. The radium clock on the dresser said five minutes after one.

I turned on my side and looked through the window. Dot had left the car's headlights on and she was walking into their glare. The pail she carried in her right hand was evidently full of water. The weight of it made her neat hips sway. She opened the black sedan door, switched on the overhead light, dug a dripping scrubbing brush out of the pail and leaned inside the car.

So that explained her antics. No doubt somebody had spilled liquid on the upholstery and she was trying to scrub it off before it dried. I dug my head into the pillow to shut out the glow of the headlights coming in through the window.

I was almost asleep when the night lamp went on in the bedroom.

"Are you awake, darling?" Dot asked.

"Um, umph, um," I mumbled, turning my head to let her know I was too sleepy for conversation.

But as nothing ever stopped Dot from talking, my desire for slumber didn't. I'd trained myself to absorb her chatter without listening to it, and that was what I did then until a startling sentence jerked me fully awake.

"I couldn't get all the blood off," she had said.

"Blood?" I breathed, opening my eyes wide. "Did you say blood?"

Dot was taking a nightgown out of a drawer. "He died on the way to the doctor," she said complacently. "I feel like a murderer."

She straightened up with the nightgown in her hand. The soft, dim night light played over her tightly and precisely formed body, and her face was as guileless as a doll's.

"Who died?" I demanded hoarsely.

"The dog, of course," she said, dropping the nightgown over her head.

I sank back on the bed. A dog, of course. Well, what had I really expected?

"I wasn't going to tell you because you're always criticizing my driving," she explained. "Like when I smashed a fender last week. But I really couldn't help what happened tonight. The dog ran right under the wheel. Then when I got home I noticed the blood in the car and I tried to wash it off, but I couldn't quite because it had dried. I decided to tell you because you'll see it tomorrow."

I was drowsy again, but puzzled. "How does blood get inside a car when you run over a dog?"

"He was still breathing, so I took him to the vet, but he was dead when I got there. The dog, I mean. The poor little thing."

She put out the light and got into bed, but that didn't stop her voice. She told me about the dollar and seventeen cents she had lost at bridge and that Ida Walker looked dowdy and Marie Cannon stunning and Edith Bauer—

"How about some sleep?" I complained.

She was quiet—for about a minute, it seemed to me. Then she was shaking me.

"Bernie," she whispered, "there's somebody sneaking about outside with a flashlight."

The radium clock said ten minutes after three, which meant that I'd actually been asleep about two hours. Dot was sitting up, and past the vague outline of her shoulder and through the window I saw a splotch of light move along the side of the car.

"Maybe he's trying to steal the car," she whispered.

"Did you leave the key in the ignition?"

It didn't surprise me when she admitted that she thought she had. Snorting, I got out of bed and went to the window. Whoever held the flashlight seemed to have lost interest in the car and was walking toward the street.

"He's going away," I said hopefully. I was a man who liked to avoid trouble.

"I wonder what he wanted."

"I know what I want," I said. "Sleep."

I had one leg on the bed when the doorbell rang. I froze half on the bed, listening. There are few things more disturbing than a doorbell ringing at three in the morning.

"That must be the thief," Dot whispered.

I roused myself. "Thieves don't ring doorbells."

"Well, it's somebody," Dot pointed out.

It certainly was somebody. The doorbell kept on ringing. I fumbled into slippers and robe, went into the living room, turned on the light, opened the front door.

The man who entered held a flashlight in his hand, so he was the same one I had seen prowling outside. He had more paunch than chest and a lumpy face.

"Mr. Bernard Hall?" he said.

I nodded. "What is it?"

He didn't answer. He stepped past me into the living room, looked it over as if he were thinking of renting it, then fixed me with rather sad eyes.

"My boy Steve is in your History class. Stephan Ricardo."

"Ah, yes," I said, using my teacher-parent manner. But that was absurd. This man hadn't got me out of bed at three in the morning to discuss his son's scholastic problems. Then I remembered what Stephen Ricardo had told me his father did for a living, and I tensed.

"You're a detective," I said.

"That's right," Ricardo massaged his jowls. "Seems there's blood in your car."

"Is that what you were looking at with your flashlight?"

He nodded. "Uh-huh. There was an attempt made to wash it off, but it was soaked into the floor rug."

At that moment Dot came into the living room. She

wore her flowered housecoat over the nightgown.

"I'm the one you want," she said. "I suppose I shouldn't have left the body in the bushes."

Ricardo pushed his hat back from his brow and blinked a couple of times. "You admit you did it, Mrs. Hall?"

"Should I have reported it to the police?" She handed him that disarming smile of hers. "The thing is, I didn't want any trouble."

"No," Ricardo said softly, "I guess you didn't want trouble." He kept looking at Dot as if he didn't quite believe she existed. "Why did you do it, Mrs. Hall?"

"It was an accident. He ran in front of the car."

Ricardo shook his head sorrowfully. "That won't get you anywhere, Mrs. Hall. His head was smashed in, but there were no other marks on his body."

"But that's impossible. I held him in my arms and his head looked all right. He seemed to be injured internally. He died before I could get him to the vet."

"The vet?" Ricardo said, blinking.

"Dr. Harrison, the veterinary on Mill Street," she explained patiently. "Where else would you take a dog?"

Ricardo opened his mouth, but he didn't say what he started to. Instead he drew in air. "Suppose, Mrs. Hall, you tell me about it."

Dot settled herself in the armchair and placidly crossed her fine legs. I stuck a cigarette between my lips and noticed that the match shook in my hand. I didn't for a moment believe that a detective would awaken and question her at three in the morning because a dog had been run over.

"I was driving to a bridge game at Marie Cannon's tonight," she said. "About two blocks from here a little black dog ran in front of the car and I couldn't stop in time. I got out and there was the poor creature in terrible agony. He was a little thing, all black with white paws and a white splotch on his face. I don't know what breed, though he had some spitz in him, because when I was a little girl I had a spitz that was the darlingest—"

"What time was this?" Ricardo broke in.

"Close to eight-thirty. Marie Cannon was anxious that we get to her house at eight-thirty, and it was just about that when I left here. I would be late, but I couldn't leave an injured dog lying in the road, so I put him in the car and drove to the vet."

"To Dr. Harrison on Mill Street," Ricardo said rather grimly. "A good seven miles away, though you were late."

"Do you know of a nearer veterinary?"

Ricardo admitted that he didn't.

"So I had no choice," Dot said. "But when I got there, I saw that the poor dog was dead, so there was no point to taking him in to Dr. Harrison. I drove back to East Billford and left the dog in some bushes beside the road."

"Just like that," Ricardo sighed.

Dot flushed guiltily. "I suppose it was a cruel thing to do, but by then it was about ten minutes after nine and the bridge game couldn't start until I got there because I made the fourth and Marie Cannon would be furious with me. And, after all, the dog was dead, wasn't he? And I did look to see if he had a license, but he didn't have even a collar. He was obviously a stray dog, and I didn't know what else to do with him."

After that gush of words there was a silence. I filled it by saying, "I suppose killing a dog should be reported to the police. That's the law, isn't it?"

"Uh-huh." He glanced at me and then returned his sad gaze to Dot. "Did you get blood on your dress when you picked him up?"

"I'm sure I didn't. One of the women at the bridge game would have noticed if I had." She frowned. "He didn't seem to bleed at all, but he must have, because I saw blood in the car when I got home hours later."

"Where did you leave the—ah—body?"

"On Pine Road, in a section where there are no houses. Just this side of that dirt road."

"Wilson Lane," he said.

"Yes, that's it. A short distance past Wilson Lane, coming toward town, there are thick bushes on the right side. That's where I left him."

Ricardo nodded and scratched his cheeks with the backs of his fingers. He was a plump man with too much waist and jowls, but the set of his lumpy face frightened me.

"You better get dressed, Mrs. Hall," he said, "and go there with me."

Her blue eyes widened. "You mean right now?"

"Right now."

"I'm going too," I said.

"Sure," Ricardo said.

We went into the bedroom to put on clothes.

"I don't understand why they make so much trouble about a dog being run over," Dot complained as she slipped her shoes on. "Of course I feel bad about it, but getting people out of bed in the middle of the night! Why doesn't he just give me a ticket and I'll pay the fine?"

I didn't say anything. My stomach was sickishly empty.

We drove in Ricardo's sedan, the three of us in the front seat.

On the way, Dot said, "I suppose Al Wilcox saw me carry the dog into the bushes. He lives down the street and knows me. I saw his white police car pass when I returned to my car."

"That's right, Mrs. Hall," Ricardo said grimly.

It was less than a mile to the spot. Three cars were parked along the side of the road, and by the light of a couple of powerful electric lanterns I saw five or six men gathered on the narrow grassy stretch between the shoulder of the road and the line of thick bushes. One of them was Al Wilcox in his policeman's uniform.

"All these men because a dog was killed!" Dot said. Even she was catching on that something bigger than that must be up.

Ricardo had no comment. He led us across the road and then I saw the long shape under the canvas. The men had become silent and were looking at Dot.

"Mrs. Hall, is this the spot?" Ricardo asked.

She nodded and slipped her hand through my arm. She frowned at the size of the thing under the canvas.

"Give her a look, Al," Ricardo said.

Wilcox bent over and gripped one end of the canvas and pulled it down. Dot uttered a shrill scream. I felt her sag against my side, clinging to my arm.

"Why that's—that's Emmett Walker!" she gasped. "I played bridge with his wife tonight."

It was Emmett Walker, all right, but no longer the handsome insurance agent Dot and I had known for years. His blond hair was matted with dried blood and some of it had run in ragged streaks over his face.

"Cover him up, Al," Ricardo said wearily. He turned to

Dot, and there was controlled fury in his voice. "He was murdered, Mrs. Hall."

"But—but where's the dog?" Dot stammered.

"There is no dog, Mrs. Hall."

"But I left him right there in those bushes."

"No, Mrs. Hall," Ricardo said. "You struck Emmett Walker over the head with something and killed him. You dragged him into your car and drove here and dragged him into the bushes. That's how the blood got in your car."

"It's not true!" Dot had recovered from the shock and was now merely indignant.

At that point I should have said something. I should have come to my wife's defense. But even if I hadn't been too choked for words, I couldn't think of any that would do any good.

Al Wilcox spoke up. "I was passing here at a few minutes after nine, Mrs. Hall, when I saw you come out of these bushes and get into your car. At two o'clock I passed this way again and by my headlights I saw what looked like a man's leg sticking out of the bushes. I investigated and found him."

"Well, I didn't do it," Dot said angrily. "Why would I want to kill Emmett Walker?"

"Suppose you tell us, Mrs. Hall."

Dot turned to me in exasperation. "You try to make him understand, darling."

I gulped air into my lungs. I said, "Of course you didn't do it," but my voice quavered.

Ricardo moved away from us to consult with the other policemen in undertones. When he returned to us, he asked Dot if the dress she had on was the one she had worn at the bridge game. She said that it was. Then he asked me for the keys to my car and handed them to Wilcox.

"Okay, let's go," Ricardo snapped.

I didn't ask him where. I knew where.

This time there were four of us in the sedan. I sat beside Ricardo, who drove, and Dot sat in the back seat with another detective. Ricardo didn't waste time. He had questions for Dot as we drove.

"Where did you say that bridge game was?"

"At Marie Cannon's house."

"Is she the wife of George Cannon, the lawyer?"

"Yes."

"Who else was there?"

"There were only four of us. Besides Marie and myself, there were Edith Bauer and Ida Walker." Her voice broke a little. "Poor Ida! Who is going to break the news to her?"

"She knows already," Ricardo said. "She didn't take the news too hard."

"They haven't got along too well lately. There were rumors that Emmett wasn't—well, exactly faithful to her." Dot leaned forward toward the back of Ricardo's neck, and her voice was breathless. "Do you think that Ida killed him?"

"I know who killed him," Ricardo said crisply.

That ended all talk until we reached the County Building, which also contained police headquarters and the county jail. Dot was taken into an office on the second floor, but I got no farther than the door.

"You might as well go home," Ricardo told me. "Your wife is being held."

"What are you going to do to her—give her the third degree?"

His lumpy face smiled a little. "We're going to question her."

"She's entitled to have a lawyer present."

"Sure." He waved a pudgy hand. "You'll find a phone booth down the hall."

I went into the booth and dialed George Cannon's number His voice was drowsy, but it got wide awake when I told him what was up.

"I'll be right there," he said.

I waited out in the hall. In ten minutes George Cannon arrived. His hair was mussed and his suit looked like a sack on his frail body, but that wasn't because he'd dressed in a hurry. He always managed to look seedy and disheveled, though he was the most prominent lawyer in East Billford.

Briefly I gave him the details. His thin mouth tightened as he listened.

"Emmett was supposed to call for Ida tonight," he told me. "She waited in my house until one o'clock and then I drove her home. I think she suspected that he was out with another woman. And all that time he was dead."

"Don't stand here talking," I said. "God knows what they're doing to Dot."

"Oh, they won't be rough with a woman. You wait here, Bernie."

He knocked at the door through which Dot had been taken and was admitted.

For a full hour I paced that lonely hall before George came out.

Glumly he shook his head. "They've taken her up to a cell through another door. She hasn't been charged yet. There are still loose ends."

"How does it look?"

"It's too soon to tell," he said, not meeting my eyes. "If the blood in the car is a dog's their circumstantial case will be shot." He patted my shoulder. "No use hanging around here. Go home and get some sleep."

He dropped me off at my house. Dawn was coming up, and in the grayness of it I saw that my car was gone. The police had taken it because it was evidence—evidence that might mean life or death.

The house was terribly empty. I went into the bedroom and there was her nightgown flung across the foot of the bed. I remembered how only a few hours ago I had watched her getting into that nightgown, and nobody could have looked less like a woman who had just murdered somebody.

She hadn't. She said so. She was flighty and talkative, but she had never before lied to me.

But she had never before had occasion to lie about murder. . . .

I tossed in bed for an hour and slept fitfully for another hour. Then the doorbell woke me. It was Herman Bauer, a fellow teacher at the high school. His wife Edith was an old friend of Dot's.

Herman, chubby and usually jolly, was now glum and embarrassed. He said that he had stopped off on his way to school to tell me that the police had questioned him and Edith.

"They got us out of bed at six-thirty this morning," Herman said. "They asked Edith about the bridge game last night. When Dot arrived, when she left, if she'd been in the house all that time, and so on. They also asked how well Dot and Emmett had known each other." He fumbled uneasily with the brim of his hat. "Neither Edith nor I mentioned that Dot used to go out with Emmett."

"That was years ago," I said. "Before Dot and I were engaged."

"Of course." Herman watched his fingers on his hat. "But the police mightn't understand." He turned to the door. "If there's anything I can do for you, let me know."

After Herman Bauer was gone, I stood in the same spot for a long time. He had it all figured out, the way everybody else figured it and the police certainly did. I couldn't know that they weren't right.

Rousing myself, I went to the phone to call the school and say that I wouldn't be in that day and maybe not for the rest of the week. Before I could start to dial the number, the phone rang.

It was George Cannon, and he said, "Bernie, can you come over to the district attorney's office right away?"

"Did anything new break?"

"Yes, but I'm afraid it's not good. The blood in your car has been analyzed." He paused and then added tonelessly, "It's human blood, and it matches Emmett Walker's blood type."

There went the last hope, I thought as I hung up. Police science had proved Dot's story about the dog a lie, and if that was false, everything else she had said was.

I dressed and left the house. The police had my car, so I had to walk to the County Building.

Detective Ricardo and George Cannon were in the district attorney's office. John Fair, the D. A., was one of those backslapping politicians who never met a voter without heartily pumping his hand, but when I entered his office he merely nodded gravely and remained in his seat.

"The analysis of the blood in your car leaves no doubt of your wife's guilt," Fair began brutally. "It took her some forty minutes to arrive at the bridge game after she left home—a distance of little over a mile. We know now that her delay was not caused by killing a dog and driving out to Dr. Harrison and back. She told the far-fetched story about the dog to explain her delay and also the blood in her car. Obviously she met Emmett Walker and killed him with a blunt instrument, probably as he was sitting in the car with her."

"What time was Walker killed?" I asked, grasping at a straw. "I mean, if he died after she arrived at the bridge game—"

Ricardo shook his heavy head. "The medical examiner can't cut it that fine. Says he thinks Walker died between nine and ten-thirty last night, and he'll give or take half an hour at either end."

"What does my wife say?" I asked weakly.

Fair shrugged irritably. "In spite of virtually conclusive evidence, she sticks to her preposterous story about the dog. A very stubborn young woman and extremely foolish." He rose and came around his desk. "Hall, I'm not out for her neck. We have learned that she and Walker were sweethearts at one time. I'm sorry to have to say this to you, but it appears that she continued to be one of his women up until last night."

"No!" I heard myself shout.

"We haven't proved it yet," Fair admitted, "but that explains her motive for killing him. Let us say that she struck him in jealous rage. In that case, I would not insist on a first-degree murder indictment. I want you to talk to her, Hall. I want you to make her see that it will be to her advantage to make a full confession."

"Prison," I said bitterly. "Is that what you offer her, years and years in prison?"

"It's better than the electric chair," Fair said softly and returned to his desk.

George Cannon hadn't said a word since I entered the office. He was our legal mind. I asked him for his opinion.

"Bernie, I'm against any deal," he declared. "I believe I can get her off free."

He believed! I looked at him standing there, seedy and slight, and at his pinched face with that perpetually hungry expression. He was East Billford's top lawyer, but it was a small city and his reputation didn't extend beyond it. He didn't think her innocent—nobody did—but he was willing to risk her life to build up his reputation in a sensational murder trial.

"I'll talk to her," I told the district attorney.

Ricardo led me upstairs to a small bare room containing only a few chairs, and left me there. A few minutes later a matron brought Dot in.

There were tired lines about her eyes and mouth, but she looked beautiful. She felt wonderful in my arms and her tremulous mouth was unendurably sweet. The electric chair, I thought dully, or years in prison that would be a living death for her.

After a minute she slipped out of my embrace. "I'd like a cigarette, darling," she said.

I lit it for her, and she sat down and crossed her legs and drew smoke into her lungs. "Darling," she said then, "they're saying terrible things about me."

She sounded indignant. Not frightened, not broken up, but merely outraged that she should be accused of having done anything wrong.

"They're even saying that Emmett was my lover," she went on angrily.

"Was he?"

When the words were out of my mouth, I hated myself for saying them. But I had to know.

Her eyebrows arched. "Darling, you don't think that too?"

"Was he, Dot?"

"Certainly not." Again that vast indignation. "Emmett meant little to me, even when I went out a few times with him before I married you."

I bent over her and took her face between my hands and looked deeply in her blue eyes. They were grave and without deceit.

"Dot," I said, "did you kill him?"

"No."

"How did the blood get in the car?"

"From the dog I ran over."

But police science had proved that a man and not a dog had bled in the car. It didn't make sense that she would tell the truth about everything but that. It was all of one piece. Frantically I wanted to believe her, but deep inside of me I didn't know.

I straightened up. She was my wife and I loved her.

"We'll fight them," I said.

When I returned to the district attorney's office, the same three men were there waiting for me.

"Well, is it a deal?" Fair asked.

"No," I said.

Ricardo sighed. Fair pounded his desk. "Very well, it will be first-degree murder then."

I turned away. George followed me out of the office and put his hand on my shoulder.

"We've got a good chance to lick them," he said. "I don't think, at any rate, that Fair can get a jury to give her the chair. We may get away with temporary insanity if she'll cooperate. I'll tell her exactly what to say on the stand, and if she sticks to it—"

"She's innocent," I said and walked away.

I was running away from his legal logic, but I couldn't run away from my hellish doubts.

Emmett Walker had had an eye for pretty women, but he had married an unattractive one. He hadn't done well as an insurance agent. Financially, being the husband of a woman with a fat bank account had paid off better.

Ida Walker was dumpy, and she had a face to match. When she admitted me into the house, she didn't give the impression of a grieving widow. She was frank about it.

"I'm not a fool," she told me. "I was aware that Emmett was constantly betraying me."

"With Dot?" I asked, looking down at the carpet.

Ida's voice was gentle. "No, Bernie. I never suspected Dot." Then she added, "But a wife is the last to know."

Or a husband, I thought, and the silence that followed was more embarrassing for me than for her. After a minute I asked her what time Emmett had been supposed to call for her last night.

"He wasn't definite," Ida said. "He told me he had work to do at his office and at eight-thirty dropped me off at Marie's in the car. He said he would try to be back before ten to watch a prize fight on the Cannons' television set. At one o'clock I gave up waiting for him and George drove me home."

"Weren't you worried when Emmett didn't show up?"

"Worried?" Ida Walker's lips curled. "Not worried in the way you mean. I assumed that he was with another woman. Then the police got me out of bed and told me he was dead."

I stood up and Ida accompanied me to the door.

"I'm a lot sorrier for Dot than for Emmett," she said. "He deserved what he got. That devil had a way with women. Even I could forgive him a lot. I was willing to accept crumbs from him, but I don't regret that he's gone."

I wondered how much she had forgiven him in the end.

Edith Bauer was Dot's best friend. She was a highstrung, delicately formed woman whose figure would be a delight in porcelain. When I told her that Dot was being charged with first-degree murder, she burst into tears.

Her husband was there. Herman lived close enough to the high school, where he taught science, to walk home for lunch, and I found them seated at the dinette table.

After Edith dried her eyes, she asked me if I would care to have a bite with them. I shook my head. I'd had no desire that morning for anything but coffee. I sat at the table with them and asked Edith if any of the four women at the bridge game last night had left for any length of time.

"You mean left the house?" she said, frowning at the question.

"At least left the room."

"Not for more than a minute or two," Edith replied. "We four were playing bridge all the time, from about a quarter to nine until almost one o'clock, when we broke off. Of course we took time off for a snack, but we were all in the same room."

"Who served refreshments?"

"Marie, naturally, but she didn't have to leave the house to do that."

"How could you start playing at a quarter to nine when Dot didn't arrive until after nine?"

"George Cannon made the fourth," she said. "He wasn't anxious to play, and when Dot arrived he gave up his seat to her and went down to the basement to work with his tools. Cabinet-making is his hobby, and he showed us the record cabinet he's building out of bleached oak. It was one of the most attractive—"

She broke off. "How can I talk about furniture at a time like this?" she wailed and started to sniffle.

I turned my attention to Herman, whose chubby face was thoughtful as he chewed his food.

"Where were you last night, Herman?" I asked.

"Home alone, catching up on my reading." He scooped up a slice of tomato from his plate. "Why is that important?"

"Because," I said carefully, "Dot wasn't the only woman at the bridge game who used to go out with Emmett Walker."

"Meaning me," Edith said. "I had quite a crush on Emmett when I was a kid." She rose quickly—too quickly, it seemed to me—to go into the kitchen for the coffeepot.

Herman had his fork poised in midair, and he studied me over it. "What are you getting at, Bernie?"

"I'm not sure," I muttered.

And that was the truth. I was groping in the dark, trying to veer guilt away from Dot to somebody else. Anybody else.

I went to see Marie Cannon. Marie was a full-bodied, slow-moving woman who caught and held men's eyes when prettier women were ignored. The housecoat she wore had a tight, high waist and a wide, low neckline that accentuated her lushness. A handkerchief was balled in her fist, and like Edith Bauer she wept at the sight of me, for she too was a close friend of Dot's.

"I can't imagine Dot killing anybody in cold blood," she said. "It must have been an accident, or temporary insanity."

I didn't argue. I had come to ask questions, and my first one was whether Dot had been greatly upset when she had arrived last night.

Marie thought that over. "She seemed somewhat out of breath, but that was all. George played out the hand before he gave up his seat to her, and as she waited she rather calmly told us that she had run over a dog." Marie unclasped her hand to stare at her moist handkerchief. "George is afraid that the fact that she had a story about killing a dog all prepared before she got here will sound bad before a jury."

Somebody came down the stairs. Marie and I turned our heads as George entered the room. He wore a faded bathrobe and flapping slippers.

"I came home for a nap," he explained. "I had only a couple of hours' sleep last night when your phone call woke me." He looked at me. "You can use some sleep too, Bernie."

Sleep? Could there be any sleep for me while Dot was shut in by four walls?

"Why would Dot have said she left a dead dog in the spot where she left the body?" I said. "If she'd killed Emmett, she would have known that his body would be found there instead."

George shrugged. "She was aware that Wilcox had seen

her come out of the bushes and that when the body was found Wilcox would put two and two together. She was frantic."

"Marie says she didn't seem very frantic when she arrived here a few minutes later."

"No, she didn't," George agreed, "but it's hard to tell with a woman like Dot. She's always breathless and bubbling and excited anyway. And she's—well, Bernie, she's lovely and charming, but her mind jumps about. I mean, that far-fetched story about a dog might have seemed like a valid explanation to her at the time, but she isn't exactly a logical person."

Not at all logical, I thought, and her flightiness used to annoy me. Now it might mean her death or imprisonment. Suddenly I was so tired that I could hardly stand. I leaned against the television cabinet, and I remembered that it was on that screen Emmett Walker had intended to see a prize fight last night. Or so Ida had told me.

I said, "The one who had most reason to kill Emmett Walker was his wife."

Marie sat down abruptly. "Yes," she whispered. "You mean before she got here last night?"

"It's possible," I said. "By the way, where was Emmett's car found?"

"At his house," George replied. "The police believe that he returned home after driving Ida here and then Dot picked him up in her car." He shook his head. "I've considered every angle too, Bernie, but they all lead to Walker's blood in your car and Dot's preposterous story about a dog."

I wasn't being logical either. I looked at Marie, who was opening her handkerchief to blow her nose, and at George, who tightened his lips glumly.

"I'll do my best to save her," George said. "The odds are that she can be got off within the law."

Odds, like gambling odds. Gambling against whether she would die or spend long years in jail or be released with the stigma of blood on her hands.

There was pity in their eyes. Pity for me, as well as for Dot. I could not stand it and I said good-bye and got out of there.

Sometimes, when I was worn out from a day of teaching and wanted quiet to read my paper, Dot's incessant and meaningless chatter would irritate me. Now the absence of her voice made the house terribly empty. I had come back home, but I couldn't endure being there without Dot. I was about to leave when the doorbell rang.

A ten-year-old boy stood there—Larry Robbins, son of the druggist who lived in the next block.

"Mr. Hall," he said, "did you see a little black dog?"

I stared at him.

"He got lost," the boy said. "I let him out for a few minutes last night and he never came back. So I'm asking all the neighbors if they saw him. Did you, Mr. Hall?"

With an effort I kept my voice calm. "What did he look like?"

"A little thing about so big. All black except for a white spot over his nose, and white paws. I got him only last week—my uncle gave him to me—and we didn't get a collar for him yet or a license. Maybe somebody thought he was a stray dog, fed him and took him in."

"What time did you let him out last night?"

"It was after eight o'clock. You didn't see him, did you?"

"Thanks, Larry," I said and patted his head.

He blinked at me. "Thanks for what, Mr. Hall?"

"Never mind," I said, and then added, "No, I didn't see your dog, Larry."

A couple of hours later, the small bulldozer I had hired arrived near the intersection of Pine Road and Wilson Lane. I'd been waiting there for some time. When the bulldozer had trundled off the truck, I told the driver where to start digging. Then I drove to the nearest phone and called Detective Ricardo at police headquarters.

"Can you come right away to where Emmett Walker's body was found last night?" I said.

"You got something, Mr. Hall?"

"I don't know," I said. "But if I have, I want you there as a witness."

I hurried back to where the bulldozer was plowing up a fifty-foot-wide area that started at the bushes along the road. Though he'd dug some three feet deep and twenty feet into the field beyond, he had so far turned up nothing but boulders. I walked beside the bulldozer blade, my feet sinking into the loose, upturned dirt.

The scooped-out area doubled in size before Ricardo showed up. His fat hips waddled as he stumbled over the chewed-up ground. He brooded at the crawling, bucking bulldozer and sighed.

"Faith moves mountains, eh, Mr. Hall?" he commented dryly.

I told him about Larry Robbins' lost dog.

"So why didn't you come to the police and let them do the digging?" he demanded.

"Because there'd be too much red tape before I got them to move, if they moved at all."

Ricardo scratched his jowls reflectively. "This field belongs to Gridley. He wouldn't like what you're doing to it."

"I obtained his permission. I'm paying him and promised to have it leveled off after—"

The driver yelled. He was climbing off the seat. Ricardo and I ran toward him. There, on the ground, half covered by dirt, was a patch of black fur. It was some fifty feet back in an almost straight line from where Walker's body had been found.

Ricardo stooped, brushed dirt away from the fur, pulled the dead animal out into the clear by one of its legs. I had never before seen that little black dog, but I had heard it described by both Dot and Larry Robbins.

Dot hadn't had a logical mind. She had only told the truth. Suddenly I was feeling fine. I had never felt better in my life.

"Do you believe now that my wife ran over a dog?"

Ricardo straightened up and dusted his hands. "Why should I?"

"W-w-why?" I stammered from sheer incredulousness. "Don't you believe what you see?"

"I see a dead dog, all right, but there are at least two things this dog didn't do. He didn't bleed in your car and he didn't leave Walker's body in the bushes. I think I know how the dog got here."

"He was buried by the murderer."

Ricardo smiled thinly. "That's what you'd like us to think. Early this morning, after you left police headquarters, you decided to try to save your wife by making her cockeyed yarn seem true. You found a little black dog and killed it and buried it here. Then you pretended to find it."

The bulldozer driver was listening open-mouthed. As for me, bitter anger had replaced my elation.

"Are you going to have the dog examined?"

"Sure, Mr. Hall, though it probably won't be possible to tell if a car or a club killed it."

There was nothing to be said. The finding of the dead dog proved everything to me and nothing to the detective. I told the bulldozer driver to shove back the dirt he had scooped out and walked to my car. The car had been returned to me a few hours ago by the police—with the bloody floor rug missing.

Ricardo moved at my side. "I guess I'd do about the same thing for my wife," he said sympathetically, "but I'd be smarter."

I whirled at the edge of the road to face him. "So you're smart! But not smart enough to see that a story can sound so far-fetched that it has to be true. My wife isn't quite the fool all of you try to make her out."

Ricardo had no comment for long moments, and his sad black eyes were reflective. He wasn't a bad guy, I thought. Not one of those bullying, blustering cops. He was trying to do what seemed to him the right thing.

"You know," he mused, looking back at the splotch of black fur on the field, "There's another answer if your wife's story about the dog is true."

"It's about time you saw it."

Suddenly he grinned at me. "You wait here. I have to take the dog's body in. Might be evidence."

He waddled over the chewed-up field. It struck me that I could accomplish more than a policeman could, and by the time he caught up with me I could hand him something. I got into my car and drove off.

Marie Cannon came to the door. Those harsh, stricken lines at the corners of her eyes and mouth had deepened within a few hours.

"George isn't home," she said.

"I'm here to see you," I said.

She led me into the living room. She sat down, keeping her full-fleshed body stiff. I stood over her.

"Marie, you've been weeping all day for Emmett Walker."

She brought the handkerchief to her nose. "Of course I'm sorry he's dead. He was a friend."

"A friend and a lover," I said. "And maybe you're weeping a little for Dot too—or for your own conscience—because you know Dot is innocent. You know that Emmett was alive at around ten o'clock, which means that Dot couldn't have killed him."

I heard a car pull into the driveway at the side of the house. Ricardo, I thought, right at my heels. I hoped that he would have sense enough to let me handle Marie.

"No, no!" Marie was saying.

"We found the dog buried near where Emmett Walker's body was found," I told her. "That proves Dot's story, and it proves that one of the people who was in this house last night killed him. They were the only ones who knew where Dot had left the dead dog."

There was a whisper of feet on the porch. Then silence. That meant that Ricardo was playing along with me. He was letting me break down Marie while he listened through the open window.

Marie was sniffling into her handkerchief.

"This is what must have happened," I went on. "Last night, you went into the kitchen to prepare refreshments. Through the window you saw Emmett Walker arrive to watch the fight on your television. You slipped out through the kitchen door to talk to him."

"I didn't kill him!" she burst out. "Let me alone!"

"You didn't kill him!" I agreed. "None of you four women in the house could have, because none of you was out of the house long enough to drive the body away. But there was a fifth person in the house—your husband."

Now, beside the edge of the curtain on one of the two windows looking out on the porch, I could see a man's hip. Ricardo was taking it all in.

"No!" Marie was wailing. "No, no!"

"Yes," I said. "It's the only possible way it could have happened. George was in the basement making a record cabinet. I've been down there a number of times. There's a ground-level window looking out to the side of the house. George saw you run out to meet Emmett. Maybe you kissed Emmett. Maybe you arranged a meeting with him. Then you returned to the kitchen and took the refreshments out to your guests. Emmett lingered outside so as not to enter the house at the same time you did and give his wife ideas. And George came out of the basement through the garage door, and in his hand he held a hammer, or whatever heavy tool he'd snatched up from his work bench."

Marie wept. In a minute she would be talking for Ricardo to hear.

I glanced toward the window and saw that Ricardo had shifted his position and that considerably more than his hip was now visible.

Only it wasn't Ricardo. The detective had a fat paunch, a padded hip. The man out there was thin, frail. George Cannon, who had seen my car parked in front of his house and had come up on the porch quietly.

All right, let him hear. Maybe he would break down when Marie did. Or he would flee and that would be as good as a confession.

I turned back to Marie. "So George killed Emmett Walker in blind, jealous fury. Then there he was with a murdered man on his hands. He had heard Dot tell that she had run over a dog and where she had left it. He saw how he could divert suspicion wholly from himself by shoving it all on Dot. He dragged the body into Dot's car, and the battered head bleeding on the floor rug fitted in with his scheme. He drove to where Dot had said she'd left the dog and found it and buried it in the fields behind the bushes and left Emmett's body there. He returned and drove Emmett's car to Emmett's house and walked back. The whole business had taken some time, but you women playing cards didn't know he was gone. Maybe he left one of his machine tools running so that you heard it upstairs and assumed he was in the basement."

"The disgrace!" Marie blubbered. "The scandal!"

And then I saw the gun. Outside the window George Cannon held it in his skinny hand against his hip. Rays from the sinking sun glinted on the barrel.

Breath clogged my throat. There was no chance in flight. Only in more words, and in not letting him realize that I knew he was there.

"So that's why you protected him," I said, "though he murdered the man you loved. You knew that George had killed him. Having seen Emmett alive and outside the house at ten, there was no other possibility. Yet you were ready to see Dot die for George's crime."

Her shoulders heaved. "George said he could get her off.

And there would have been a frightful scandal if George had gone on trial. Everybody would have known that Emmett had been my—my—" Her voice went completely to pieces.

I looked at Marie as I spoke, but actually my words were directed to the man outside with the gun. "The police know the truth," I said. "When they found the dog's body, the pieces fell into place. With your evidence, there will be no doubt of his guilt. The police are on their way now to—"

Outside, somebody yelled. The man at the window jerked around, and all of George Cannon's slight body became visible. He held the muzzle of his gun against his temple.

The sound of the shot wasn't very loud. Then he crumpled out of sight below the window sill, and I saw Ricardo running up the porch steps.

I dashed out to the porch. Ricardo was looking down at the dead man.

"Shot himself when he saw me," Ricardo said. "Guess he thought I was coming to arrest him."

"Yes," I muttered. "I made him think so."

He raised angry black eyes to me. "Why didn't you wait for me?"

"Does it matter now?" I said, turning away from George Cannon's body.

Inside the house, Marie was sobbing brokenly.

"I guess not," Ricardo said softly. He went into the house.

I walked as far as the porch steps so that I would not be too near the dead man. In a little while, I thought, I would be bringing Dot home.

And I would buy Larry Robbins another dog.

The Twenty Friends of William Shaw

RAYMOND E. BANKS

It isn't often that a butler calls at my house. Even less often is he carrying a lunch basket. But I admitted Higgins because he worked for William Shaw, and William Shaw once—well, he had done me a great favor.

Higgins was affably formal, and conveyed his employer's respects. I brought out a bottle of my best wine, still remembering my indebtedness—because William Shaw was an old and true friend.

"Bring me up to date," I said. "I haven't seen Mr. Shaw for a long time. Well, since he was—"

"Since his marriage," said Higgins quietly. I had always admired Higgins' firm jaw and precise manner of speech. He was the kind of butler who could competently direct the affairs of the moment by just the right kind of smile or frown. Now his face was absolutely set in stone—a man committed to a purpose. "Since his marriage," he repeated.

"Grace Shaw was rather—I mean, after the marriage her presence put a kind of damper on the old crowd," I said.

"Mr. Shaw had very few weaknesses," said Higgins. "His wife was one of them. An older man—a younger woman. His later years have been difficult."

Higgins moved his lunch basket delicately with the pointed toe of his conservative black shoe. "Because of Mr. Shaw's desire to help people he found himself in a bad position," said Higgins. "There is little left of what was once a large estate. Divorce was out of the question, since Mrs. Shaw would certainly have settled for no less than most of it."

I recalled the last time I'd been to the Shaws'—the stunning sparkle of the necklace Grace Shaw had worn and the way she had caressed it against her white throat.

"Most certainly out of the question," I said, unconsciously imitating a little Higgins' extremely precise English. It was hard not to imitate that dry forceful voice.

"Deserting one's wife and going into hiding leaves much to be desired," Higgins went on. "Principally, it cuts a man off from his friends—and Mr. Shaw always lived for his friends."

"We had some great times," I said. "Before."

"Furthermore, accidents are hard to explain," Higgins went on.

I found myself staring now at the basket with a growing interest and distaste.

I shuddered, but it may have been the wine. It sparkled blood-red in Higgins' pale fingers as he lifted his glass to the sunlight. My picture window was open, and a strong earth smell, a smell of spring and flowers lingered in the room—a time of hope and reawakening.

"You have a fine home here," said Higgins, looking around. "You've done well. Mr. Shaw will be delighted to know that you have done so well."

"I was once at the point of killing myself," I said. There was something about him that invited confidence. "I was a pretty dismal failure. I was broke, without friends or family. I was also seriously ill, and I didn't even have enough money to buy drugs to ease my pain. I went up into the Hollywood Hills. To that big sign up there that spells out H-O-L-L-Y-W-O-O-D across the face of the hills. People used to jump off that sign, you know."

"But then you met Mr. Shaw," Higgins said, smiling a little.

"Turning point," I said. "He was a stranger—he owed me nothing. But he spent a great deal of time and money in getting me back on my feet. I shall never forget it."

"Of course you shan't," said Higgins. "Mr. Shaw has at least twenty friends like you. People who were in desperate circumstances when he found them."

Higgins edged the basket further from himself, and closer to me. His smile increased in warmth and understanding.

"I always hoped—I could repay him in some way," I said.

"Mr. Shaw never expects repayment when he helps people," said Higgins. "Still, there is a little matter in which you might be able to help him."

"Well, if there's anything—" I let the words hang, because the smile was no longer in evidence. He looked suddenly almost forbidding.

"Unfortunately the man who has been always the soul of kindness may well die at the hands of the state," said Higgins, his eyes clouded. "However, it is probable that Grace Shaw's disappearance will cause no great comment. She has disappeared before—once with a sailor for a two-week affair in San Diego. Another time, I believe, with a truck driver."

"I had heard she had her faults," I said.

Higgins' perfectly tailored shoulders shrugged. "This time—who knows? Butcher, baker, candlestick maker. She is gone and Mr. Shaw looks and acts twenty years younger—as if a great weight had been lifted from his shoulders. Of course, there is her pesky brother trying to make trouble. But Mr. Shaw won't have him around, now that Grace has gone."

He finished his wine and rose. "Mr. Shaw's best and closest friends are all helping him. Perhaps twenty or so—the ones who owed him the most. I trust we can count on you."

"I—I . . ."

But Higgins bowed, and moved to the door. "I wouldn't delay if I were you," he said. "The weather is warm and the dry ice won't last long. Good day, Mr. Benson. But not goodbye. Mr. Shaw will soon have one of his old-time get-togethers. A sort of celebration, and you and your wife are most cordially invited."

I walked him to the door. I accompanied him across the small porch, down the walk and to the door of the Rolls. "I haven't had much experience in these matters," I protested.

"Mr. Goodlace went fishing on a deep-sea boat," said Higgins. "Mr. Al Drayton was putting in a brick patio. Eileen Wilson found her garden needed new rose bushes—the deep-rooted kind. One's mind can conceive of many possibilities." Higgins grasped my hand and smiled. "Take care of yourself, Mr. Benson. You look pale. I suggest you lie down and rest for a few moments. Mr. Shaw always considered you one of his staunchest—"

The Rolls was gone.

I have never been one to do much work in the yard. But the family was away, and it was a sunny afternoon, so I went out into the garden with the shovel, leaving the basket in the garage. The first patch of ground resisted any considerable digging, but I found another softer spot by a patch of hyacinths.

Soon I became aware of another presence at my side.

"What are you doing?" said the small child—a boy. He was watching me with serious eyes.

I thought of a possible range of replies but settled for a simple one. "Digging," I said.

"Digging what?" the neighbor's child asked. It was Danny, the curious one, already launched on a lifetime of gossip.

"A hole," I said, beginning to sweat even though I was barely more than six inches down.

This went on until he learned I was planting a rose bush.

"My mom doesn't plant rose bushes that deep," he said, hard and suspicious. Normally, he had an attractive young face full of intelligence. Today his eyes looked close-set, his mouth sneering.

"You may be right," I said abandoning the project. With thirty-five children loose in the neighborhood, it didn't seem precisely the right way to proceed. There wasn't much time left as my wife would be back at five, and my son Timmy at six.

Many persons do not know the virtues of the modern-day city dump. The old-fashioned dump with its shacks and its islands of rubble, some burning, surrounded by railroad tracks and inhabited by derelicts is a thing of the past.

The dump near my home is run by the JHK Construction Company. It's a tract of low land that is being slowly filled, and will eventually become the construction site for a long row of forty-thousand-dollar homes. It is surrounded by a high wire fence, and has a polite attendant who checks in the customers at the entrance. Beyond the gate are several winding roads, and a fresh site for the dumping activities of the day. As the trucks drive up, a bulldozer snorts, scrambles, whines and keens, mashing and crushing the discarded goods into the rich, black earth.

Beneath its blade, mixed into a permanent cocktail with the earth are old bedsprings, clippings from the gardeners' trucks, papers, bottles, clothes and furniture. After the bulldozer passes over there is nothing left but churned up ground with a leavening of mashed paper or wood or green branches. Tomorrow another layer will cover this layer, then another, and eventually still another. Archeologists of the future will have to take the twentieth century bulldozer into account.

Once inside the gate you join a procession of trucks, with a few plain cars with trailers moving to the dumping spot of the day. You back in a few feet from where the bulldozer works and deposit your stuff. There are always some coming in and dumping in the shadow of the bulldozer and as it eternally groans away, the dumping spot changes.

I had filled the car with the accumulation of the garage, which I had been promising to do for months anyway. Things that the weekly pickup service wouldn't touch. Higgins' basket looked innocent enough in the symphony of crud I carried.

I was about to back into a dumping spot when I took note of a car only one truck ahead of me. It looked disturbingly familiar. I hadn't seen Ben Jackson for a couple of years, but there was no doubt that the car was sporting one of Ben's distinctive paint jobs. And there was good old Ben himself, one of William Shaw's best friends, jockeying the vehicle into position to dump.

I parked out of the line and went over to see him. He wasn't glad to see me, and when I surveyed his trailer full of dumpings, I could understand why. Higgins had been going the rounds that Saturday.

"I thought of it first!" he cried.

"It is a large dump," I said. "A very large dump."

He was a fat, balding man with vague brown eyes. He waved at the three dump attendants who were busily engaged in picking over the materials left by the trucks.

"One could get by. Two—that would look suspicious," he said.

"I can't help it," I said. "There are only so many places."

That was when the accident happened. I don't know whether I slipped, or whether Ben stumbled against me. But there was a truck hurrying in alongside of him; it caught me and knocked me flat on the ground.

Things went whirly-whirly for a while. I heard voices

and the large, kind face of William Shaw came down out of the sky and smiled and thanked me for the kind of assistance I was giving him. I tried to protest that I really couldn't help my bungling when I felt the strong fingers of the dump attendant pressing me into the seat behind the wheel of my car.

"Your friend helped you empty your stuff and left. You better go home now," said the attendant, wetting his lips nervously.

His nervousness wasn't hard to understand. I might be badly hurt. I might even require ambulance attention. Later I might sue the dump. On the whole, he thought it better if I left. So I did. The aspects of danger on my end were strong enough to get me out of there in a hurry.

Safe on the road, I looked in the back seat to be sure all the stuff had vanished. The dump stuff was gone, and that pleased me. But resting on the back seat were two baskets instead of my original one.

I tried to think but didn't get very far. I was still dazed and aching from the dump accident, although I had suffered no permanent damage. I decided to go on home and look up Ben Jackson's address and go calling on him with a crowbar.

My anger lasted all the way home, until I drove up in front of the house and saw, on my front porch, a too-familiar basket. The note attached to it was written in a flowing feminine hand:

"You'll remember," it said, "Sarah King, a good friend of William Shaw's. I haven't seen you for a long time, Mr. Benson, but I know you can help me. I am practically a shut-in these days and live in an apartment. I know you are a gentleman and will be glad to help an old lady who doesn't get around much. Would you please take care of Mr. Shaw's rose bush for me? You live closest to me of all his friends and have a nice, big yard." It was signed *Sarah King*.

I hurried into the house. I was panicky. True, William Shaw had saved my life, and helped start me on a useful career. But there were limits to gratitude.

The phone rang with a monotonous petulance which suggested it had been ringing for a long time. It was Charles Moriseau, Grace Shaw's brother. I recognized the defensively belligerent voice before he'd spoken three words.

"Have you seen Grace Shaw?" he asked.

"No," I said, trying to make my voice sound natural though fear kept tightening my throat. I had not seen her. I had seen only some white packages, securely wrapped and tied, in three baskets. So at least I wasn't lying.

"My illustrious brother-in-law claims she's disappeared," said Moriseau. "I suspect foul play by some of his crude friends."

I had a mental picture of Moriseau as I'd last seen him. The too-cultured voice, the moist hands, the balding head, the fish-pale blue eyes that peered suspiciously on all the human race. I remembered Shaw's gracious good humour and fun. I began to get a little angry.

"Your sister hasn't a very conspicuous reputation as a stay-at-home," I said.

"I think there's something odd going on," he said. "I may be coming to see you and some of his so-called friends —with the police."

"Any day, old man, any day," I said and hung up. That settled it. *I* wasn't going to be Moriseau's tool for destroying my good friend, William Shaw.

A week went by. I was ready for the expected visit of Moriseau and a heavy-footed policeman. I was completely ready, and even had an alibi for that particular Saturday afternoon. No one came; there was nothing in the papers. Once I drove by the Shaw place in Bel Air, one of the largest mansions. I saw only a uniformed Pinkerton man patrolling the grounds. I tried to call Higgins but the phone was answered by a professional guard who said nobody was home.

The tension lasted, but nothing disturbing happened. However, my wife complained about my peevishness and one night I threw an old shoe at my son.

Relief finally came. I received a note addressed by Higgins which read: "Mr. Shaw is taking a trip to Europe, after a trying winter. He will see all his old friends when he returns in the fall."

So that ended it. William Shaw was going to be all right, and I and the rest of us had nothing to worry about.

• • •

"Why do you swerve whenever you see a police car?"

my wife asked. "Have you been cheating on your income tax again?"

Why, indeed, I wondered. To hell with waiting until fall! I wanted to be doubly sure that no policeman would come knocking at my door.

I bought a bottle of champagne and forced my way into the Shaw mansion. Again I met the imperturbable Higgins and told him about the call from Moriseau.

Higgins smiled his quiet smile. "We have nothing to fear, Mr. Benson. In fact, the trip to Europe was deliberately planned to put an end to Moriseau's staying here, now that his sister has—ah—run off with another disreputable man. There were just the four of us—Mr. and Mrs. Shaw, Mr. Moriseau and myself. Mrs. Shaw is gone. Now we can close the house and he will have to leave. But there'll be good times for all of us again in the fall!"

I pointed to some luggage lined up in the hall—two large trunks, and several women's suitcases. "It looks as if I barely made it," I said. "Maybe I'd better give this champagne to William and be on my way."

Higgins shook his head. "That wouldn't be wise, Mr. Benson. We have convinced Moriseau that his sister has run off. It wouldn't look right if he saw familiar faces—faces of the old crowd—appearing so soon."

"I see your logic," I said, setting the bottle on the luggage. "Give my regards to William."

I stood at the dock in Los Angeles Harbor watching the departure of the big liner for Hawaii. It had been all too easy to discover the booking in the name of "Mr. and Mrs. Higgins." I saw them briefly at the rail, but took great care to make sure they wouldn't see me.

Charles Moriseau was there, grinning and waving up at his sister and his new brother-in-law. With William dead and buried by his twenty best friends, they had it made. Grace could support both Higgins and Charles in good style, because none of them spent with the generosity that poor William had displayed all of his life. Her necklace sparkled from her smooth throat, Higgins' teeth glistened in the sun as he hugged her and laughed a happy, unbutler-like laugh.

I left and sent my telegrams to the harbor police, telling them anonymously what they'd find in the three baskets in he Higgins' stateroom. Baskets that I'd kept on ice in a riendly butcher shop while wracking my poor, unimaginaive brain in an unnecessary effort to get myself off the well-known hook.

Higgins had planned the murder well, and executed the removal of the body neatly—the practical butler to the end. Higgins had made only one slip—a slip he couldn't help. There were three men and one woman living in that mansion. The woman was supposed to be dead—yet in the luggage he'd prepared for the trip to Europe (and wasn't it obvious that they'd take reservations in the opposite direction?) Higgins had a set of women's luggage.

Now no proper butler of Higgins' ability would send two males, his master and himself, off to Europe with a lady's luggage!

The Other Hangman

CARTER DICKSON

Why do they electrocute 'em instead of hanging 'em in Pennsylvania? What (said my old friend, Judge Murchison, dexterously hooking the spittoon closer with his foot) do they teach you in these new-fangled law schools, anyway? Because that, son, was a murder case! It turned the Supreme Court whiskers grey to find a final ruling, and for thirty years it's been argued about by lawyers in the back room of every saloon from here to the Pacific coast. It happened right here in this county—when they hanged Fred Joliffe for the murder of Randall Fraser.

It was in '92 or '93; anyway, it was the year they put the first telephone in the courthouse, and you could talk as far as Pittsburgh except when the wires blew down. Considering it was the county seat, we were mighty proud of our town (population 3,500). The hustlers were always bragging about how thriving and growing our town was, and we had just got to the point of enthusiasm where every ten years we were certain the census-taker must have forgotten half our population. Old Mark Sturgis, who owned the *Bugle Gazette* then, carried on something awful in an editorial when they printed in the almanac that we had a population of only 3,263. We were all pretty riled about it.

We were proud of plenty of other things, too. We had good reason to brag about the McClellan House, which was the finest hotel in the county; and I mind when you could get room and board, with apple pie for breakfast every morning, for two a week. We were proud of our old county families, that came over the mountains when Braddock's army was scalped by the Indians in 1775, and settled down in log huts to dry their wounds. But most of all we were proud of our legal batteries.

Son, it was a grand assembly! Mind, I won't say that all

of 'em were long on knowledge of the Statute Books; but they knew their Blackstone and their Greenleaf on Evidence, and they were powerful speakers. And there were some—the top-notchers, full of graces and book-knowledge and dignity—who were hell on the exact letter of the law. Scotch-Irish Presbyterians, all of us, who loved a good debate and a bottle o' whisky. There was Charley Connell, a Harvard graduate and the district attorney, who had fine hands, and wore a fine high collar, and made such pathetic addresses to the jury that people flocked for miles around to hear him; though he mostly lost his cases. There was Judge Hunt, who prided himself on his resemblance to Abe Lincoln, and in consequence always wore a frock coat and an elegant plug hat. Why, there was your own grandfather, who had over two hundred books in his library, and people used to go up nights to borrow volumes of the encyclopaedia.

You know the big stone courthouse at the top of the street, with the flowers round it, and the jail adjoining? People went there as they'd go to a picture show nowadays; it was a lot better, too. Well, from there it was only two minutes' walk across the meadow to Jim Riley's saloon. All the legal cronies gathered there—in the back room of course, where Jim had an elegant brass spittoon and a picture of George Washington on the wall to make it dignified. You could see the footpath worn across the grass until they built over that meadow. Besides the usual crowd, there was Bob Moran, the sheriff, a fine, strapping big fellow, but very nervous about doing his duty strictly. And there was poor old Nabors, a big, quiet, reddish-eyed fellow, who'd been a doctor before he took to drink. He was always broke, and he had two daughters—one of 'em consumptive—and Jim Riley pitied him so much that he gave him all he wanted to drink for nothing. Those were fine, happy days, with a power of eloquence and theorizing and solving the problems of the nation in that back room, until our wives came to fetch us home.

Then Randall Fraser was murdered and there was hell to pay.

Now if it had been anybody else but Fred Joliffe who killed him, naturally we wouldn't have convicted. You can't do it, son, not in a little community. It's all very well to talk about the power and grandeur of justice, and sounds fine in a speech. But here's somebody you've seen walking the streets about his business every day for years; and you know when his kids were born, and saw him crying when one of 'em died; and you remember how he loaned you ten dollars when you needed it . . . Well, you can't take that person out in the cold light of day and string him up by the neck until he's dead. You'd always be seeing the look on his face afterwards. And you'd find excuses for him no matter what he did.

But with Fred Joliffe it was different. Fred Joliffe was the worst and nastiest customer we ever had, with the possible exception of Randall Fraser himself. Ever seen a copperhead curled up on a flat stone? And a copperhead's worse than a rattlesnake—that won't strike unless you step on it, and gives warning before it does. Fred Joliffe had the same brownish colour and sliding movements. You always remembered his cart through town—he had some sort of rag-and-bone business, you understand—you'd see him sitting up there, a skinny little man in a brown coat, peeping round the side of his nose to find something for gossip. And grinning.

It wasn't merely the things he said about people behind their backs. Or to their faces, for that matter, because he relied on the fact that he was too small to be thrashed. He was a slick customer. It was believed that he wrote those anonymous letters that caused . . . but never mind that. Anyhow, I can tell you this little smirk did drive Will Farmer crazy one time, and Will did beat him within an inch of his life. Will's livery stable was burned down one night about a month later with eleven horses inside, but nothing could ever be proved. He was too smart for us.

That brings me to Fred Joliffe's only companion—I don't mean friend. Randall Fraser had a harness-and-saddle store in Market Street, a dusty place with a big dummy horse in the window. I reckon the only thing in the world Randall liked was that dummy horse, which was a dappled mare with vicious-looking glass eyes. He used to keep its mane combed. Randall was a big man with a fine moustache, and a horseshoe pin in his tie, and sporty checked clothes. He was buttery polite, and mean as sin. He thought a dirty trick or a swindle was the funniest joke he ever heard. But the women liked him—a lot of them, it's no use denying, sneaked in at the back door of that harness store. Randall itched to tell it at the barber shop, to show what fools they were and how virile he was, but he had to be careful. He and Fred Joliffe did a lot of drinking together.

Then the news came. It was in October, I think, and I heard it in the morning when I was putting on my hat to go down to the office. Old Withers was the town constable then. He got up early in the morning, although there was no need for it, and when he was going down Market Street in the mist about five o'clock he saw the gas still burning in the back room of Randall's store. The front door was wide open. Withers went in and found Randall lying on a pile of harness in his shirt-sleeves, his forehead and face bashed in with a wedging-mallet. There wasn't much left of the face, but you could recognize him by his moustache and his horseshoe pin.

I was in my office when somebody yelled up from the street that they found Fred Joliffe drunk and asleep in the flour mill, with blood on his hands and an empty bottle of Randall Fraser's whisky in his pocket. He was still in bad shape, and couldn't walk or understand what was going on, when the sheriff—that was Bob Moran I told you about—came to take him to the lock-up. Bob had to drive him in his own rag-and-bone cart. I saw them drive up Market Street in the rain, Fred lying in the back of the cart all white with flour, and rolling and cursing. People were very quiet. They were pleased, but they couldn't show it.

That is, all except Will Farmer, who had owned the livery stable that was burnt down.

"Now they'll hang him," says Will. "Now, by God, they'll hang him."

It's a funny thing, son, I didn't realize the force of that until I heard Judge Hunt pronounce sentence after the trial. They appointed me to defend him, because I was a young man without any particular practice, and somebody had to do it. The evidence was all over town before I got a chance to speak with Fred. You could see he was done for. A scissors-grinder who lived across the street (I forget his name now) had seen Fred go into Randall's place about eleven o'clock. An old couple who lived up over the store had heard 'em drinking and yelling downstairs. At near on midnight they'd heard a noise like a fight and a fall—but they knew better than to interfere. Finally, a couple of farmers driving home from town at midnight had seen Fred stumble out of the front door, slapping his clothes and wiping his hands on his coat like a man with delirium tremens.

I went to see Fred at the jail. He was sober, although he jerked a good deal. Those pale eyes of his were as poisonous as ever. I can still see him sitting on the bunk in his cell, sucking a brown paper cigarette, wriggling his neck, and jeering at me. He wouldn't tell me anything, because he said I would go and tell the judge if he did.

"Hang me?" he says, and wrinkled his nose and jeered again. "Hang me? Don't you worry about that, mister. Them so-and-so's will never hang me. They're too much afraid of me, them so-and-so's are. Eh, mister?"

And the fool couldn't get it through his head right up until the sentence. He strutted away in court making remarks, and threatening to tell what he knew about people, and calling the judge by his first name. He wore a new dickey shirt-front he bought to look spruce in.

I was surprised how quietly everybody took it. The people who came to the trial didn't whisper or shove; they just sat still as death and looked at him. All you could hear was a kind of breathing. It's funny about a courtroom, son. It has its own particular smell, which won't bother you unless you get to thinking about what it means, but you notice worn places and cracks in the walls more than you would anywhere else. You would hear Charley Connell's voice for the prosecution, a little thin sound in a big room, and Charley's footsteps creaking. You would hear a cough in the audience, or a woman's dress rustle, or the gas-jets whistling. It was dark in the rainy season, so they lit the gas-jets by two o'clock in the afternoon.

. . .

The only defense I could make was that Fred had been too drunk to be responsible, and remembered nothing of that night (which he admitted was true). But, in addition to being no defense in law, it was a terrible frost besides. My own voice sounded wrong. I remember that six of the jury had whiskers, and six hadn't, and Judge Hunt, up on the bench with the flag draped on the wall behind his head, looked more like Abe Lincoln than ever. Even Fred Joliffe began to notice. He kept twitching round to look at the people, a little uneasy-like. Once he stuck out his neck at the jury and screeched: "Say something, cantcha? Do something, cantcha?"

They did.

When the foreman of the jury said, "Guilty of murder in the first degree," there was just a little noise from those people. Not a cheer or anything like that. It hissed out all together, only once, like breath released, but it was terrible to hear. It didn't hit Fred until Judge Hunt was halfway through pronouncing sentence. Fred stood looking round with a wild, half-witted expression until he heard Judge Hunt say, "And may God have mercy on your soul." Then he burst out, kind of pleading and kidding as though this was carrying the joke too far. He said, "Listen now, you don't mean that, do you? You can't fool me. You're only Jerry Hunt. I know who you are. You can't do that to me." All of a sudden he began pounding the table and screaming, "You ain't really a-going to hang me, are you?"

But we were.

The date of the execution was fixed for the twelfth of November. The order was all signed. ". . . within the precincts of the said county jail, between the hours of eight and nine A.M., the said Frederick Joliffe shall be hanged by the neck until he is dead; an executioner to be commissioned by the sheriff for this purpose, and the sentence to be carried out in the presence of a qualified medical practitioner; the body to be interred . . ." And the rest of it. Everybody was nervous. There hadn't been a hanging since any of that crowd had been in office, and nobody knew how to go about it exactly. Old Doc Macdonald, the coroner, was to be there and of course they got hold of Reverend Phelps the preacher and Bob Moran's wife was going to cook pancakes and sausage for the last breakfast. Maybe you think that's fool talk. But think for a minute of taking somebody you've known all your life, and binding his arms one cold morning, and walking him out in your own back yard to crack his neck on a rope—all religious and legal, with not a soul to interfere. Then you begin to get scared of the powers of life and death, and the thin partition between.

Bob Moran was scared white for fear things wouldn't go

off properly. He had appointed big, slow-moving, tipsy Ed Nabors as hangman. This was partly because Ed Nabors needed the fifty dollars and partly because Bob had a vague idea that an ex-medical man would be better able to manage an execution. Ed had sworn to keep sober. Bob Moran said he wouldn't get a dime unless he was sober, but you couldn't always tell.

Nabors seemed in earnest. He had studied up the matter of scientific hanging in an old book he borrowed from your grandfather, and he and the carpenter had knocked together a big, shaky-looking contraption in the jail yard. It worked all right in practice, with sacks of meal. The trap went down with a boom that brought your heart up in your throat. But once they allowed for too much spring in the rope, and it tore a sack apart. Then old Doc Macdonald chipped in about that fellow John Lee, in England—and it nearly finished Bob Moran.

That was late on the night before the execution. We were sitting round the lamp in Bob's office, trying to play stud poker. There were tops and skipping-ropes, all kinds of toys, all over that office. Bob let his kids play in there—which he shouldn't have done, because the door out of it led to a corridor of cells with Fred Joliffe in the last one. Of course the few other prisoners, disorderlies and chicken-thieves and the like, had been moved upstairs. Somebody had told Bob that the scent of an execution affects 'em like a cage of wild animals. Whoever it was, he was right. We could hear 'em shifting and stamping over our heads, and one colored boy singing hymns all night long.

Well, it was raining hard on the thin roof. Maybe that was what put Doc Macdonald in mind of it. Doc was a cynical old devil. When he saw that Bob couldn't sit still, and would throw in his hand without even looking at the buried card, Doc says:

"Yes, I hope it'll go off all right. But you want to be careful about that rain. Did you read about that fellow they tried to hang in England—and the rain had swelled the boards so's the trap wouldn't fall? They stuck him on it three times, but still it wouldn't work."

Ed Nabors slammed his hand down on the table. I reckon he felt bad enough as it was, because one of his daughters had run away and left him, and the other was dying of consumption. But he was twitchy and reddish about the eyes. He hadn't had a drink for two days, although there was a bottle on the table. He says:

"You shut up or I'll kill you. Damn you, Macdonald," he says, and grabs the edge of the table. "I tell you nothing can go wrong. I'll go out and test the thing again, if you'll let me put the rope round your neck."

And Bob Moran says, "What do you want to talk like that for anyway, Doc. Ain't it bad enough as it is?" he says. "Now you've got me worrying about something else," he says. "I went down there a while ago to look at him, and he said the funniest thing I ever heard Fred Joliffe say. He's crazy. He giggled and said God wouldn't let them so-and-so's hang him. It was terrible, hearing Fred Joliffe talk like that. What time is it, somebody?"

It was cold that night. I dozed off in a chair, hearing the rain, and that animal-cage shuffling upstairs. The colored boy was singing that part of the hymn about while the nearer waters roll, while the tempest still is high.

They woke me about half past eight to say that Judge Hunt and all the witnesses were out in the jail yard, and they were ready to start the march. Then I realized that they were really going to hang him after all. I had to join behind the procession as I was sworn, but I didn't see Fred Joliffe's face and I didn't want to see it. They had given him a good wash, and a clean flannel shirt that they tucked under at the neck. He stumbled coming out of the cell, and started to go in the wrong direction, but Bob Moran and the constable each had him by one arm. It was a cold, dark, windy morning. His hands were tied behind.

The preacher was saying something I couldn't catch, and everything went off smoothly enough until they got half-way across the jail yard. It's a pretty big yard. I didn't look at the contraption in the middle, but at the witnesses standing over against the wall with their hats off. But Fred Joliffe did look at it, and went down flat on his knees. They hauled him up again. I heard them keep on walking, and go up the steps, which were creaky.

I didn't look at the contraption until I heard a thumping sound, and we all knew something was wrong.

Fred Joliffe was not standing on the trap, nor was the bag pulled over his head, although his legs were strapped.

He stood with his eyes closed and his face toward the pink sky. Ed Nabors was clinging with both hands to the rope, twirling round a little and stamping on the trap. It didn't budge. Just as I heard Ed crying something about the rain having swelled the boards, Judge Hunt ran past me to the foot of the contraption.

Bob Moran started cursing pretty obscenely. "Put him on and try it, anyway," he says, and grabs Fred's arm. "Stick that bag over his head and give the thing a chance."

"In His name," says the preacher pretty steadily, "you'll not do it if I can help it."

Bob ran over like a crazy man and jumped on the trap with both feet. It was stuck fast. Then Bob turned round and pulled an Ivor-Johnson .45 out of his hip-pocket. Judge Hunt got in front of Fred, whose lips were moving a little.

"He'll have the law, and nothing but the law," says Judge Hunt. "Put that gun away, you lunatic, and take him back to the cell until you can make the thing work. Easy with him, now."

To this day I don't think Fred Joliffe had realized what happened. I believe he only had his belief confirmed that they never meant to hang him after all. When he found himself going down the steps again, he opened his eyes. His face looked shrunken and dazed-like, but all of a sudden it came to him in a blaze.

"I knew them so-and-so's would never hang me," says he. His throat was so dry he couldn't spit at Judge Hunt, as he tried to do, but he marched straight and giggling across the yard. "I knew them so-and-so's would never hang me," he says.

We all had to sit down a minute, and we had to give Ed Nabors a drink. Bob made him hurry up, although we didn't say much, and he was leaving to fix the trap again when the courthouse janitor came bustling into Bob's office.

"Call," says he, "on the new machine over there. Telephone."

"Lemme out of here!" yells Bob. "I can't listen to no telephone calls now. Come out and give us a hand."

"But it's from Harrisburg," says the janitor. "It's from the Governor's office. You got to go."

"Stay here, Bob." says Judge Hunt. He beckons to me. "Stay here, and I'll answer it," he says. We looked at each other in a queer way when we went across the Bridge of Sighs. The courthouse clock was striking nine, and I could look down into the yard and see people hammering at the trap. After Judge Hunt had listened to that telephone call he had a hard time putting the receiver back on the hook.

"I always believed in Providence, in a way," says he, "but I never thought it was so person-like. Fred Joliffe is innocent. We're to call off this business," says he, "and wait for a messenger from the Governor. He's got the evidence of a woman . . . Anyway, we'll hear it later."

Now, I'm not much of a hand at describing mental states, so I can't tell you exactly what we felt then. Most of all was a fever and horror for fear they had already whisked Fred out and strung him up. But when we looked down into the yard from the Bridge of Sighs we saw Ed Nabors and the carpenter arguing over a crosscut saw on the trap itself, and the blessed morning light coming up in glory to show us we could knock that ugly contraption to pieces and burn it.

The corridor downstairs was deserted. Judge Hunt had got his wind back, and, being one of those stern elocutionists who like to make complimentary remarks about God, he was going on something powerful. He sobered up when he saw that the door to Fred Joliffe's cell was open.

"Even Joliffe," says the judge, "deserves to get this news first."

But Fred never did get the news, unless his ghost was listening. I told you he was very small and light. His heels were a good eighteen inches off the floor as he hung by the neck from an iron peg in the wall of the cell. He was hanging from a noose made in a child's skipping-rope; black-faced dead already, with the whites of his eyes showing in slits, and his heels swinging over a kicked-away stool.

. . .

No, son, we didn't think it was suicide for long. For a little while we were stunned, half crazy, naturally. It was like thinking about your troubles at three o'clock in the morning.

But you see, Fred's hands were still tied behind him. There was a bump on the back of his head, from a hammer that lay beside the stool. Somebody had walked in there with the hammer concealed behind his back, had stunned Fred when he wasn't looking, had run a slip-knot in that skipping-rope, and jerked him up a-flapping to strangle there. It was the creepiest part of the business, when we'd got that through our heads, and we all began loudly to tell each other where we'd been during the confusion. Nobody had noticed much. I was scared green.

When we gathered round the table in Bob's office, Judge Hunt took hold of his nerve with both hands. He looked at Bob Moran, at Ed Nabors, at Doc Macdonald, and at me. One of us was the other hangman.

"This is a bad business, gentlemen," says he, clearing his throat a couple of times like a nervous orator before he starts. "What I want to know is, who under sanity would strangle a man when he thought we intended to do it anyway, on a gallows?"

Then Doc Macdonald turned nasty. "Well," says he, "if it comes to that, you might in-quire where that skipping-rope came from to begin with."

"I don't get you," says Bob Moran, bewildered-like.

"Oh, don't you," says Doc, and sticks out his whiskers. "Well, then, who was so dead set on this execution going through as scheduled that he wanted to use a gun when the trap wouldn't drop?"

Bob made a noise as though he'd been hit in the stomach. He stood looking at Doc for a minute, with his hands hanging down—and then he went for him. He had Doc back across the table, banging his head on the edge, when people began to crowd into the room at the yells. Funny, too; the first one in was the jail carpenter, who was pretty sore at not being told that the hanging had been called off.

"What do you want to start fighting for?" he says, fretful-like. He was bigger than Bob, and had him off Doc with a couple of heaves. "Why didn't you tell me what was going on? They say there ain't going to be any hanging. Is that right?"

Judge Hunt nodded, and the carpenter—Barney Hicks, that's who it was; I remember now—Barney Hicks looked pretty peevish, and says:

"All right, all right, but you hadn't ought to go fighting all over the joint like that." Then he looks at Ed Nabors.

"What I want is my hammer. Where's my hammer, Ed? I been looking all over the place for it. What did you do with it?"

Ed Nabors sits up, pours himself four fingers of rye, and swallows it.

"Beg pardon, Barney," says he in the coolest voice I ever heard. "I must have left it in the cell," he says, "when I hanged Fred Joliffe."

Talk about silences! It was like one of those silences when the magician at the Opera House fires a gun and six doves fly out of an empty box. I couldn't believe it. But I remember Ed Nabors sitting big in the corner by the barred window, and his shiny black coat and string tie. His hands were on his knees, and he was looking from one to the other of us, smiling a little. He looked as old as the prophets then, and he'd got enough liquor to keep the nerve from twitching beside his eye. So he just sat there, very quietly, shifting the plug of tobacco around in his cheek, and smiling.

"Judge," he says in a reflective way, "you got a call from the Governor at Harrisburg, didn't you? Uh-huh. I knew what it would be. A woman had come forward, hadn't she, to confess Fred Joliffe was innocent and she had killed Randall Fraser? Uh-huh. The woman was my daughter. Jessie couldn't face telling it here, you see. That was why she ran away from me and went to the Governor. She'd have kept quiet if you hadn't convicted Fred."

"But why? . . ." shouts the judge. "Why? . . ."

"It was like this," Ed goes on in that slow way of his. "She'd been on pretty intimate terms with Randall Fraser, Jessie had. And both Randall and Fred were having a whooping lot of fun threatening to tell the whole town about it. She was pretty near crazy, I think. And, you see, on the night of the murder Fred Joliffe was too drunk to remember anything that happened. He thought he had killed Randall, I suppose, when he woke up and found Randall dead and blood on his hands.

"It's all got to come out now, I suppose," says he, nodding. "What did happen was that the three of 'em were in that back room, which Fred didn't remember. He and Randall had a fight while they were baiting Jessie. Fred whacked him hard enough with that mallet to lay him out, but all the blood he got was from a big splash over Randall's eye. Jessie . . . Well, Jessie finished the job when Fred ran away, that's all."

"But, you damned fool," cries Bob Moran, and begins to pound the table, "why did you have to go and kill Fred when Jessie had confessed?"

"You fellows wouldn't have convicted Jessie, would you?" says Ed, blinking at us. "No. But, if Fred had lived after her confession, you'd have had to, boys. That was how I figured it out. Once Fred learned what did happen, that he wasn't guilty and she was, he'd never have let up until he'd carried that case to the Superior Court out of your hands. He'd have screamed all over the state until they either had to hang her or send her up for life. I couldn't stand that. As I say, that was how I figured it out, although my brain's not so clear these days. So," says he, nodding and leaning over to take aim at the cuspidor, "when I heard about that telephone call, I went into Fred's cell and finished my job."

"But don't you understand," says Judge Hunt, in the way you'd reason with a lunatic, "that Bob Moran will have to arrest you for murder, and . . ."

It was the peacefulness of Ed's expression that scared us then. He got up from his chair, and dusted his shiny black coat, and smiled at us.

"Oh no," says he very clearly. "That's what you don't understand. You can't do a single damned thing to me. You can't even arrest me."

"He's bughouse," says Bob Moran.

"Am I?" says Ed affably. "Listen to me. I've committed what you might call a perfect murder, because I've done it legally . . . Judge, what time did you talk to the Governor's office, and get the order for the execution to be called off? Be careful now."

And I said, with the whole idea of the business suddenly hitting me:

"It was maybe five minutes past nine, wasn't it, Judge? I remember the courthouse clock striking."

"I remember it too," says Ed Nabors. "And Doc Macdonald will tell you Fred Joliffe was dead before ever that clock struck nine. I have in my pocket," says he, unbuttoning his coat, "a court order which authorizes me to kill Fred Joliffe, by means of hanging by the neck—which I did—between the hours of eight and nine in the morning—which I also did. And I did it in full legal style before the order was countermanded. Well?"

Judge Hunt took off his stovepipe hat and wiped his face with a bandana. We all looked at him.

"You can't get away with this," says the judge, and grabs the sheriff's order off the table. "You can't trifle with the law in that way. And you can't execute sentence alone. Look here! 'In the presence of a qualified medical practitioner.' What do you say to that?"

"Well, I can produce my medical diploma," says Ed, nodding again. "I may be a booze hoister, and mighty unreliable, but they haven't struck me off the register yet . . . You lawyers are hell on the wording of the law," says he admiringly, "and it's the wording that's done for you this time. Until you get the law altered with some fancy words, there's nothing in that document to say that the doctor and the hangman can't be the same person."

After a while Bob Moran turned round to the judge with a funny expression on his face. It might have been a grin.

"This ain't according to morals," says he. "A fine citizen like Fred shouldn't get murdered like that. It's awful. Something's got to be done about it. As you said yourself this morning, Judge, he ought to have the law and nothing but law. Is Ed right, Judge?"

"Frankly, I don't know," says Judge Hunt, wiping his face again. "But, so far as I know, he is. What are you doing, Robert?"

"I'm writing him out a check for fifty dollars," says Bob Moran, surprised-like. "We got to have it all nice and legal, haven't we?"

Dune Roller

JULIAN MAY

There were only two who saw the meteor fall into Lake Michigan, long ago. One was a Pottawatomie brave hunting rabbits among the dunes on the shore; he saw the fire-streak arc down over the water and was afraid, because it was an omen of ill favor when the stars left the heaven and drowned themselves in the Great Water. The other who saw was a sturgeon who snapped greedily at the meteor as it fell—quite reduced in size by now—to the bottom of the fresh water sea. The big fish took it into his mouth and then spat it out again in disdain. It was not good to eat. The meteor drifted down through the cold black water and disappeared. The sturgeon swam away, and presently, he died. . . .

Dr. Ian Thorne squatted beside a shore pool and netted things. Under the sun of late July, the lake waves were sparkling deep blue far out, and glass-clear as they broke over the sandbar into Dr. Thorne's pool. A squadron of whirligig beetles surfaced warily and came toward him leading little v-shaped shadow wakes along the tan sand bottom. A back-swimmer rowed delicately out of a green cloud of algae and snooped around a centigrade thermometer which was suspended in the water from a driftwood twig.

3:00 P.M., wrote Dr. Thorne in a large, stained notebook. *Air temp* 32, *water temp*—he leaned over to get a better look at the thermometer and the back-swimmer fled—28. *Wind, light variable; wave action, diminishing. Absence of drifted specimens.* He dated a fresh sheet of paper, headed it *Fourteenth Day,* and began the bug count.

He scribbled earnestly in the sun, a pleasant-faced man of thirty or so. He wore a Hawaiian shirt and shorts of delicious magenta color, decorated with most unbotanical green hibiscus. An old baseball cap was on his head.

He skirted the four-by-six pool on the bar side and noted that the sand was continuing to pile up. It would not be long before the pool was stagnant, and each day brought new and fascinating changes in its population. *Gyrinidae, Hydrophilidae,* a *Corixa* hiding in the rubbish on the other end. Some kind of larvae beside a piece of water-logged board; he'd better take a specimen or two of that. *L. intacta* sunning itself smugly on the thermometer.

The back-swimmer, its confidence returned, worked its little oars and zig-zagged in and out of the trash. *N. undulata,* wrote Dr. Thorne.

When the count was finished, he took a collecting bottle from the fishing creel hanging over his shoulder and maneuvered a few of the larvae into it, using the handle of the net to herd them into position.

And then he noticed that in the clear, algae-free end of the pool, something flashed with a light more golden than that of mere sun on water. He reached out the net to stir the loose sand away.

It was not a pebble or a piece of chipped glass as he had supposed; instead, he fished out a small, droplike object shaped like a marble with a tail. It was a beautiful little thing of pellucid amber color, with tiny gold flecks and streaks running through it. Sunlight glanced off its smooth sides, which were surprisingly free of the surface scratches that are the inevitable patina of flotsam in the sand-scoured dunes.

He tapped the bottom of the net until the drop fell into an empty collecting bottle and admired it for a minute. It would be a pretty addition to his collection of Useless Miscellanea. He might put it in a little bottle between the tooled brass yak bell and the six-inch copper sulfate crystal.

He was collecting his equipment and getting ready to leave when the boat came. It swept up out of the north and nosed in among the sand bars offshore, a dignified, forty-foot Matthews cruiser named *Carlin,* which belonged to his friend, Kirk MacInnes.

" 'Hoy, Mac!" Dr. Thorne yelled cordially. "Look out for the new bar the storm brought in!"

A figure on the flying bridge of the boat waved briefly and howled something unintelligible around a pipe clamped in its teeth. The cruiser swung about and the mutter of her motors died gently. She lay rocking in the little waves a few hundred feet offshore. After a short pause a yellow rubber raft dropped over the stern.

Good old Mac, thought Thorne. The little ex-engineer with that Skye terrier moustache and the magnificent boat visited him regularly, bringing the mail and his copy of the *Biological Review,* or bottled goods of a chemistry designed to prevent isolated scientists from catching cold. He was a frequent and welcome visitor, but he had always come alone.

Previous to this.

"Well, well," said Dr. Thorne, and then looked again.

The girl was sitting in the stern of the raft while MacInnes paddled deftly, and as they drew closer Thorne saw that her hair was dark and curly. She wore a spotless white playsuit, and a deep blue handkerchief was knotted loosely around her throat. She was looking at him, and for the first time he had qualms about the Hawaiian shorts.

The yellow flank of the raft grated on the stony beach. MacInnes, sixty and grizzled, a venerable briar between his teeth, climbed out and wrung Thorne's hand.

"Brought you a visitor this time, Ian. Real company. Jeanne, this gentleman in the shorts and fishing creel is Dr. Ian Thorne, the distinguished writer and lecturer. He writes books about dune ecology, whatever that is. Ian, my niece, Miss Wright."

Thorne murmured politely. Why, that old scoundrel. That sly old dog. But she was pretty, all right.

"How engaging," smiled the girl. "An ecologist with a leer."

Dr. Thorne's face abruptly attempted to adopt the protective coloration of his shorts. He said, "We're really not bad fellows at heart, Miss Wright. It's the fresh air that gives us the pointed ears."

"I see," she said, in a tone that made Thorne wonder just how much she saw. "Were you collecting specimens here today, Dr. Thorne?"

"Not exactly. You see, I'm preparing a chapter on the ecology of beach pool associations, and this little pool here is my guinea pig. The sand bar on the lake side will grow until the pool is completely cut off. As its stagnation increases, progressive forms of plant and animal life will inhabit it—algae, beetles, larvae, and so forth. If we have calm weather for the next few weeks, I can get an excellent cross section of the plant-animal societies which develop in this type of an environment. The chapter on the pool is one in a book I'm doing on ecological studies of the Michigan State dunes."

"All you have to do is charge him up," MacInnes remarked, yawning largely, "and he's on the air for the rest of the day." He pulled the raft up onto the sand and took out a flat package. "I brought you a present, if you're interested."

"What is it? The mail?"

"Something a heck of a lot more digestible. A brace of sirloins. I persuaded Jeanne to come along today to do them up for us. I've tasted your cooking."

"I can burn a chop as well as the next man," Thorne protested with dignity. "But I think I'll concede the point. I was finished here. Shall we go right down to the shack? I live just down the shore, Miss Wright, in a place perched on top of a sand dune. It's rugged but it's home."

MacInnes chuckled and led the way along the firm damp sand near the water's edge.

In some places the tree-crowned dunes seemed to come down almost to the beach level. Juniper and pines and heavy undergrowth were the only things holding the vast creeping monster which are the traveling dunes. Without their green chains, they swept over farms and forests, leaving dead trees and silver-scoured boards in their wake.

The three of them cut inland and circled a great narrow-necked valley which widened out among the high sand hills. It was a barren, eery place of sharp, wind-abraded stumps and silent white spaces.

"A sand blow," said Thorne. "The winds do it. Those dunes at the end of the valley in there are moving. See the dead trees? The hills buried them years ago and then moved on and left these skeletons. These were probably young oaks."

"Poor things," said the girl, as they moved on.

Then the dismal blow was gone, and green hills with scarcely a show of sand towered over them. At the top of the largest stood Thorne's lodge, its rustic exterior blending inconspicuously into the conifers and maples which surrounded it on three sides. The front of the house was banked with yew and prostrate juniper for sand control.

A stairway of hewn logs came down the slope of the dune. At its foot stood a wooden bench, a bright green pump, and an old ship's bell on a pole.

"A dunes doorbell!" Jeanne exclaimed, seizing the rope.

"Nobody home yet," Thorne laughed, "but that's the shack up there."

"Yeah," said MacInnes sourly. "And a hundred and thirty-three steps to the top."

Later, they sat in comfortable rattan chairs on the porch while Thorne manipulated siphon and glasses.

"You really underestimate yourself, Dr. Thorne," the girl said. "This is no shack, it's a real home. A lodge in the pines."

"Be it ever so humble," he smiled. "I came up here to buy a two-by-four cabin to park my typewriter and microscopes in, and a guy wished this young chalet off on me."

"The view is magnificent. You can see for miles."

"But when the wind blows a gale off the lake, you think the house is going to be carried away! It's just the thing for my work, though. No neighbors, not many picnickers, not even a decent road. I have to drive my jeep down the beach for a couple of miles before I can hit the cow path leading to the county trunk. No telephones, either. And I have my own little generating plant out back, or there wouldn't be any electricity."

"No phone?" Jeanne frowned. "But Uncle Kirk says he talks to you every day. I don't understand."

"Come out here," he invited mysteriously. "I'll show you something."

He led the way to a tiny room with huge windows which lay just off the living room. Radio equipment stood on a desk and lined the walls. A large plaster model of a grasshopper squatting on the transmitter rack wore a pair of headphones.

"Ham radio used to be my hobby when I was a kid," he said, "and now it keeps me in touch with the outside world. I met Mac over the air long before I ever saw him in the flesh. You must have seen his station at home. And I think he even has a little low power rig in the cruiser."

"I've seen that. Do you mean he can talk to you any time he wants to?"

"Well, it's not like the telephone," Thorne admitted, "the

other fellow has to be listening for you on your frequency. But your uncle and I keep a regular schedule every evening and sometimes in the morning. And hams in other parts of the country are very obliging in letting me talk to my friends and colleagues. It works out nicely all the way around."

"Uncle Kirk had represented you as a sort of scientific anchorite," she said, lifting a microphone and running her fingers over the smooth chrome. "But I'm beginning to think he was wrong."

"Maybe," he said quietly. "Maybe not. I manage to get along. The station is a big help in overcoming the isolation, but—there are other things. Shall we be getting back to the drinks?"

She put down the microphone and looked at him oddly. "If you like. Thank you for showing me your station."

"Think nothing of it. If you're ever in a jam, just howl for W8-Dog-Zed-Victor on ten meters."

"All right," she said to him. "If I ever am." She turned and walked out of the door.

The casual remark he had been about to make died on his lips, and suddenly all the loneliness of his life in the dunes loomed up around him like the barren walls of the sand blow. And he was standing there with the dead trees all around and the living green forever out of reach. . . .

"This Scotch tastes like iodine," said MacInnes from the porch.

Thorne left the little room and closed the door behind him. "It's the only alcohol in the house, unless you want to try my specimen pickle," said Thorne, dropping back into his chair. "As for the flavor—you should know. You brought the bottle over yourself last week."

The girl took Thorne's creel and began to arrange the bottles in a row on the table. Algae, beetles, and some horrid little things that squirmed when she shook them. Ugh.

"What's this?" she asked curiously, holding up the bottle with the amber drop.

"Something I found in my beach pool this afternoon. I don't know what it is. Rock crystal, perhaps, or somebody's drowned jewelry."

"I think it's rather pretty," she said admiringly. "It reminds me of something, with that little tail. I know—Prince Rupert drops. They look just like this, only they're a bit smaller and have an air bubble in them. When you crack the little tail off them, the whole drop flies to powder." She shrugged vaguely. "Strain, or something. I never saw one that had color like this, though. It's almost like a piece of Venetian glass."

"Keep it, if you like," Thorne offered.

MacInnes poured himself another finger and thumb of Scotch and scrupulously added two drops of soda. In the center of the table, the small amber eye winked faintly in the sunlight.

Tommy Dittberner liked to walk down the shore after dinner and watch the sand toads play. There were hundreds of them that came out to feed as soon as dusk fell—little silvery-gray creatures with big jewel eyes, that swam in the mirror of the water or sat quietly on his hand when he caught them. There were all sizes, from big fellows over four inches long to tiny ones that could perch comfortably on his thumbnail.

Tommy came to Port Grand every August, and lived in a resort near the town. He knew he was not supposed to go too far from the cottage, but it seemed to him that there were always more and bigger toads just a little farther down the shore.

He would go just down to that sand spit, that was all. Well, maybe to that piece of driftwood down there. He wasn't lost, like his mother said he would be if he went too far. He knew where he was; he was almost to the Bug Man's house.

He was funny. He lived by himself and never talked to anyone—at least that's what the kids said. But Tommy wasn't too sure about that. Once last week the Bug Man and a pretty lady with black hair had been hiking in the dunes near Tommy's cottage and Tommy had seen him kiss her. Boy, that had been something to tell the kids!

Here was the driftwood, and it was getting dark. He had been gone since six o'clock, and if he didn't get home, Mom was going to give it to him, all right.

The toads were thicker than ever, and he had to walk carefully to avoid stepping on any of them. Suddenly he saw one lying in the sand down near the water's edge. It was on its back and kicked feebly. He knelt down and peered closely at it.

"Sick," he decided, prodding it with a finger. The animal winced from his touch, and its eyes were filmed with pain. But it wasn't dead yet.

He picked it up carefully in both hands and scrambled over the top of the low shore dune to the foot of the great hill where the Bug Man lived.

Thorne opened the door to stare astonished at the little boy, and wondered whether or not to laugh. Sweat from the exertion of climbing the one hundred and thirty-three steps had trickled down from his hair, making little stripes of cleanness on the side of his face. His T-shirt had parted company from the belt of his jeans. He held out the toad in front of him.

"There's this here toad I found," he gasped breathlessly. "I think it's sick."

Without a word, Thorne opened the door and motioned the boy in. They went into the workroom together.

"Can you fix it up, mister?" asked the boy.

"Now, I'll have to see what's wrong first. You go wash your face in the kitchen and take a Coke out of the icebox while I look it over."

He stretched it out on the table for examination. The abdomen was swollen and discolored, and even as he watched it the swelling movement of the floor of its mouth faltered and stopped, and the animal did not move again.

"It's dead, ain't it?" said a voice behind Thorne.

"I'm afraid so, sonny. It must have been nearly dead when you found it."

The boy nodded gravely. He looked at it silently for a moment, then said: "What was the matter with it, mister?"

"I could tell if I dissected it. You know what that is, don't you?" The boy shook his head. "Well, sometimes by looking inside of the sick thing that has died, you can find out what was wrong. Would you like to watch me do it?"

"I guess so."

Scalpel and dissecting needle flashed under the table light. Thorne worked quickly, glancing at the boy now and then out of the corner of his eye. The instruments slicked within the redness of the incision and parted the oddly darkened and twisted organs.

Thorne stared. Then he arose and smiled kindly at the young face before him. "It died of cessation of cardiac activity, young fellow. I think you'd better be heading for home now. It's getting dark and your mother will be worried about you. You wouldn't want her to think anything had happened to you, would you? I didn't think so. A big boy like you doesn't worry his mother."

"What's a cardiac?" asked the boy, looking back over his shoulder at the toad as Thorne led him out.

"Means 'pertaining to the heart,' " said Thorne. "Say, I'll tell you what. We'll drive home in my jeep. Would you like that?"

"I guess so."

The screen door slammed behind them. The kid would forget the toad quickly enough, Thorne told himself. He couldn't have seen what was inside it anyway.

In the lodge later, under the single little light, Thorne preserved the body of the toad in alcohol. Beside him on the table gleamed two tiny amber drops with tails which he had removed from the seared and ruptured remains of the toad's stomach.

The marine chronometer on the wall of Thorne's amateur station read five-fifteen. His receiver said to him:

"I have to sign off now. The missus is hollering up that she wants me to see to the windows before supper. I'll look for you tomorrow. This is W8GB over to W8DVZ, and W8GB is out and clear. Good night, Thorne."

Thorne said, "Good night, Mac. W8DVZ out and clear," and let the power die in his tubes.

He lit a cigarette and stood looking out of the window. In the blue sky over the lake hung a single, giant white thunderhead; it was like a marble spray billow, ponderous and sullen. The rising wind slipped whistling through the stiff branches of the evergreen trees on the dune, and dimly, through the glass, he could hear the sound of the waves.

He moped around inadequately after supper and waited for something to happen. He typed up the day's notes, tidied the workroom, tried to read a magazine, and then thought about Jeanne. She was a sweet kid, but he didn't love her. She didn't understand.

The sand walls seemed to be going up around him again. He wasn't among the dead trees—he was one of them, rooted in the sand with the living greenness stripped from his heart.

Oh, what the hell. The magazine flew across the room

and disappeared behind the couch in a flutter of white pages.

He stormed into the workroom, bumped the shelves, and set the specimens in their bottles swaying sadly to and fro. In the second bottle from the end, right-hand side, was a toad. In the third were two small amber drops with tails, whose label said only:

YOU TELL ME—8/5/57

Interest stirred. Now, there was a funny thing. He had almost forgotten. The beads, it would seem, had been the cause of the toad's death. They had evidently affected the stomach and the surrounding tissues before they had had a chance to pass through the digestive tract. Fast work. He picked up the second bottle and moved it gently. The pale little thing inside rotated until the incision, with all the twisted organs plainly visible inside, faced him. Willy Seppel would have liked to see this; too bad he was across the state in Ann Arbor.

Idly, Thorne toyed with the idea of sending the pair of drops to his old friend. They were unusual looking—he could leave the label on, write a cryptic note, and fix Seppel's clock for putting the minnows in his larvae pail on their last field trip together.

If he hurried, he could get the drops off tonight. There was a train from Port Grand in forty-five minutes. As for the storm, it was still a long way off; he doubted that it would break before nightfall. And the activity would do him good.

He found a small box and prepared it for the mails. Where was that book of stamps? The letter to Seppel: he slipped a sheet of paper into the typewriter and tapped rapidly. String—where was the string? Ah, here it was in the magazine rack. Now a slicker, and be sure the windows and doors are locked.

His jeep was in a shed at the bottom of the dune, protected by a thick scrub of cottonwood and cedar. Since there was no door, Thorne had merely to reverse gears, shoot out, swing around, and roar over the improvised stone drive to the hard, wet sand of the beach. Five miles down the shore was an overgrown but still usable wagon trail which led to the highway.

The clouds were closing ranks in the west as Dr. Thorne and his jeep disappeared over the crest of a tall dune.

Mr. Gimpy Zandbergen, gentleman of leisure, late of the high sea and presently of the open road, was going home. During a long and motley life, Mr. Zandbergen had wandered far from his native lakes to sail on more boisterous waters; but now his days as an oiler were over, and there came into his heart a nostalgic desire to see the fruit boats ship out of Port Grand once more. Since he possessed neither the money for a bus ticket home, nor the ambition to work to obtain it, he pursued his way via freight cars and such rides as he was able to hook from kindly disposed truck drivers.

His last ride had carried him to a point on the shore highway some miles south of his goal, at which he had regrettably disputed the intrinsic worth of the Detroit Tigers and had been invited to continue his journey on foot. But Mr. Zandbergen was a simple soul, so he merely shrugged his shoulders, fortified himself from the bottle in his pocket, and trudged along.

It was hot, though, as only Michigan in August can be, and the sun baked the concrete and reflected off the sand hills at the side of the road. He paused, pulled a blue bandanna handkerchief from his pocket, and mopped his balding head under his cap. He thought longingly of the cool dune path which he knew lay on the other side of the forest, toward the lake.

It had been a long time, but he knew he remembered it. It would lead to Port Grand and the fruit boats, and would be refreshingly cool.

When the storm came, Mr. Zandbergen was distinctly put out. He had not seen the gathering storm through the thick branches, and when the sky darkened, he assumed that it was merely one of the common summer sun showers and hoped for a quick clearing.

He was disturbed when the big drops continued to pelt down among the oak trees. He was annoyed as his path led him out between the smaller and less sheltering evergreens. He swore as the path ended high on a scrubby hill.

Lightning cut the black clouds and Mr. Zandbergen broke into a lope. He had taken the wrong turning, he knew that now. But he recognized this shore. He dimly remembered a driftwood shanty which lay near an old wagon road somewhere around here. If he made that, he might not get too wet after all.

He could see the lake now. The wind was raging and tearing at the waves, whipping the once placid waters of Michigan into black fury. Mr. Zandbergen shuddered in the driving rain and fled headlong down a dune. Great crashes of thunder deafened him and he could hardly see. Where was that road?

A huge sheet of lightning lit the sky as he struggled to the top of the next dune. There it was! The road was down there! And trees, and the shanty, too.

He went diagonally across the dune in gigantic leaps, dodging the storm-wracked trees and bushes. The wind lulled, then blasted the branches down ferociously, catching him a stinging blow across the face. He tripped, and with an agonized howl began to roll straight down the bare face of the sand hill. He landed in a prickly juniper hedge and lay, whimpering and cursing weakly, while the rain and wind pounded him.

The greenery ripped from the trees stung into him viciously as he tried to rise, gave up, and tried again. On the black beach several hundred feet away, waves leaped and stretched into the sky.

Then came another lull and a light appeared out in the lake. It rose and fell in the surf and in a few moments the flattened and horrified little man on the shore could see what it was. A solemn thunderclap drowned out his scream of terror.

Shouting wordless things, he stumbled swaying to his feet and clawed through the bushes to fall out onto the road. It saw him! He was sure it saw him! He struggled along on his knees in the sand for a short distance before he fell for the last time.

The wind shrilled again in the trees, but the fury of the storm had finally passed. The rain fell down steadily now on the sodden sand dunes, and dripped off the cottonwood branches onto the quiet form of Mr. Zandbergen, who would not see the fruit boats go out again after all.

The sheriff was a conversational man. "Now I've lived on the lake for forty years," he said to Thorne, "but never —*never* did I see a storm like today's. No sir!" He turned to his subordinate standing beside him. "Regular typhoon, eh, Sam? I guess we won't be forgetting that one in a hurry."

Dr. Thorne, at any rate, would not forget it. He could still hear in his mind the thunder as it had rolled away off over the dunes, and see the flaring white cones of his headlights cutting out his way through the rain. He had gone slowly over the sliding wet sand of the wagon road on the way home, but even at that he had almost missed seeing it. He remembered how he had thought it was a fallen branch at first, and how he got out of the car then and stood in the rain looking at it before he wrapped his slicker around it and drove back to town.

And now the rain had stopped at last, and the office of the Port Grand physician who was the county medical examiner was neat, dim, and stuffy with the smell of pharmaceuticals and wet raincoats. Over the other homely odors hung the stench of burnt flesh.

Snip, went the physician's bandage shears through charred cloth. Thorne lit a cigarette and inhaled, but the sharp, sickening other smell remained in his nostrils.

"According to his Seamen's International card, he was George Zandbergen of Port Grand," said the sheriff to Sam, who carefully transcribed this information in his notebook. To Thorne he said, "Did you know him, mister?"

Thorne shook his head.

"I remember him, Peter," said the physician, experimentally determining the stiffness of the dead fingers before him. "Appendicitis in 1946. Left town after that. I think he used to be an oiler on the *Josephine Temple* in the fruit fleet. I'll have a file on him around somewhere."

"Get that, Sam," said the sheriff. He turned to Thorne, standing awkwardly at the foot of the examination table. "We'll have to have your story for the record, of course. I hope this won't take too long. Start at the beginning, please."

Gulping down his nervousness and revulsion, Thorne told of returning from town about nine o'clock and finding the corpse of a man lying in the middle of a deserted side road. Dr. Thorne recalled puzzling at the condition of the body, for although it had been storming heavily at the time, portions of the body had been burned quite black.

Thorne had found something at the scene also, but failing to see that it had any connection with the matters at hand, prudently kept his discovery to himself. The sheriff would hardly be interested in it, he told himself, but nevertheless he hoped that the bulge it made in his pocket wasn't too noticeable.

Officer Sam Stern made the last little tipped-v that stood for a period in his transcription and looked nervously about him. His chief peered approvingly—even if uncomprehendingly—at the notes and then said:

"How does it look, doctor?"

"Third degree burns on fifty percent of the body area, seared to the bone in some parts of the face and about the right scapula. How did you say he was lying when you found him, Mr. Thorne?"

"In an unnatural kind of sprawled position, on the right side."

The physician yawned, rummaged in a cabinet and produced a sheet with which he covered the charred body. "Pretty obvious, Peter, with these burns and all. Verdict is accidental death. The poor devil was struck by lightning. Time of death was about eight P.M." He tucked the sheet securely around the head. "That lightning's pretty odd stuff, now. Can blow the soles off a man's shoes without scratching him, or generate enough heat to melt metal. You never know what tricks it's going to play. Take this guy here: one side of him's broiled black and the other's not even singed. Well, you never know, do you?"

He picked up his phone and conversed briefly with the local undertaking parlor. When negotiations for the disposition of the unfortunate Mr. Zandbergen had been completed, he replaced the receiver and shuffled toward the door. Thorne could see that he had bedroom slippers on under his rubbers.

"You can finish up tomorrow, Peter," he resumed. "My wife was kinda peeved at me coming out this way. You know how women are, ha-ha. Good night to you, Mr. Thorne. I think there's an old overcoat in that closet I could let you take. You'll be wanting to send yours to the cleaners."

There was a genial guffaw from the sheriff. "We won't keep you any longer tonight, Mr. Thorne. Just let me know how I can get in touch with you."

"Through Kirk MacInnes on River Road," said Thorne. "He'll be glad to contact me through his amateur station." He edged through the door into the quiet night. The sheriff came close behind.

"So you're a ham, eh?" he said warmly. "Well, can you tie that! I used to have a ticket myself in the old days."

Polite noises. How about that? Kindred souls. Sorry about all this sloppy business, old man. Tough luck you had to be the one to find him. Really nothing, old man. *Why* didn't he stop talking? The weight in Thorne's pocket seemed to grow.

"You know, I'll be dropping in to see your rig some one of these days if you don't mind. I'll bet you could use a little company out there in the dunes, eh?"

No, why should he mind? Delighted, old man. Any time at all.

The thing in his pocket seemed to sag to his ankles. It would rip the pocket and fall out. And it had bits of charred cloth on it. Why didn't they go? They couldn't possibly suspect that he hadn't—

Oh, yes, he was on ten meters. Phone. Oh, the sheriff had done c.w. on 180? Well, wasn't that nice.

They walked to the cars under the big old elm trees that lined the comfortable street. A few stars came out and down where the street dead-ended into the river, they could see lights moving toward the deepwater channel that connected the river with the lake.

"Well, good night, Sheriff," Thorne said. "Good night, Mr. Stern. I hope next time we'll meet under more pleasant circumstances."

"Good night, Mr. Thorne," said Sam, who was thoroughly bored with talk he didn't understand, and anxious to get home to his wife and baby.

The police got into their car and drove off. Thorne sat quietly behind the wheel of the jeep until he was sure they were gone, then gingerly removed the weight from his pocket and unwrapped the handkerchief that covered it.

This one was the size of a closed fist and irregular in shape. He had found it flattened under the black char that had once been a man's shoulder, glowing with a bright yellow light in its heart. It looked the same as the three small drops he had previously seen, but he saw that what he had mistaken for golden flecks inside of it was really a fine network of metallic threads which formed a web apparently imbedded a few centimeters below the thing's surface.

The damn thing, he thought. There was something funny about it, all right.

Around him, the lights of the quiet houses were going out one by one. It was eleven o'clock. A few wet patches still glistened on the street under the lamps, and a boat motor on the river pulsed, then stilled.

Thorne looked around him quickly, then got out of the car and laid the thing on the curb. The wet leaves in the gutter below it reflected yellow faintly.

It was funny that a mere matter of shape could change his feeling toward it so radically. The smaller drops had been rather beautiful in their droplike mystery, but this one, although it was made of the same wonderful stuff, had none of the beauty. The irregular cavity in its side that would fit a human shoulder blade made it a thing sinister; the dried blood and ashes made it monstrous.

He took a tire iron out of the tool kit and tapped the glowing thing experimentally. It was certainly stronger than it looked, at any rate. When harder taps failed to crack it, he raised the iron and brought it down with all his strength. The tool bounced, skidded, and chipped the concrete curbstone, but the thing flew undamaged into the gutter.

Thorne bent down and poked it incredulously. And suddenly, with a cry of agony, he dropped the tire iron. It was hot! The tool arced down and lay sizzling sullenly among the little drops of water that still clung to the grass blades. His hand—He clenched his teeth to keep from crying out.

But the glowing thing in the gutter was not hot. Steam rose from the iron in the grass, but the little rivulets bathing the glowing thing were cool. He seemed to remember something, but then the shocked numbness coming over his hand took his attention and he forgot it again.

Down among the leaves and trash, the thing that was not shattered by the strength of Dr. Thorne grew, momentarily, more golden; and with a deliberate, liquid ripple the ugly bulges on its surface smoothed and it assumed the perfect drop shape of its predecessors.

200000 AU PLUS PLENTY WATTS. TELL ME PRETTY MAIDEN ARE THERE ANY MORE AT HOME LIKE YOU? ARRIVE NOON THURSDAY. LOVE. SEPPEL.

"You think you're pretty smart, don't you?" said Thorne.

"Yep," said Willy Seppel smugly, smirking around the edge of his beer. He put down the glass and the smirk expanded to a grin. "Smart enough to see what those drops were that you sent me for a gag. That was a great little trick of yours, you know. I was all set to throw them out after reading that note of yours. The only thing that saved them was Archie Deck. He thought they might be Prince Rupert drops and tried to crack the tails off with a file."

"Aha," said Dr. Thorne.

Seppel looked at him with bright blue, innocent eyes. He was a large, pink-faced, elegantly dressed man with an eagle-beak nose and a crown of fine, blond hair.

"You don't have to look at me like that," said Thorne. "I've been able to find out a little bit more about them myself."

"Tell me," said the pink face complacently.

"They generate heat. And I found out the same way as Archie Deck probably did." He gestured with one bandaged hand. "Only I managed it the hard way." He swept up the empty glasses and beer bottles with a crash and disappeared into the kitchen. His voice continued distantly:

"I found those two I sent you inside the stomach of a toad. Or at least what was left of the stomach of a toad. Look in the lab room, the big shelf; second bottle from the end on the right-hand side."

Wiping his good hand on his trousers, he returned to Seppel, who stood looking thoughtfully into the toad's bottle. "It ate the drops," Thorne said shortly.

"Mm—yes," he mused. "The digestive juices might very possibly be able to—"

"Come on, Willy. What is it?"

"You were almost right when you said it generated heat," Willy said. "I brought one of them here to show you." He left the room and returned in a minute with a large cowhide briefcase.

"This thing's in a couple of pieces," Seppel apologized.

"You'll have to wait until I set it up. Have you got a step-down transformer?"

Thorne nodded and fetched it from the bookcase.

"Now this little drop here may look like a bead, but it has some singular properties." He removed the thing from a box which had been heavily sealed and padded, and set it in a nest of gray, woolly stuff in the middle of the table.

"It gives off long infrared, mostly stacked up around 200,000 Angstroms. But their energy is way out of proportion from what you'd expect from the equation. This little gadget is something Deck and I rigged up to measure it crudely. Essentially, it's a TC130X couple hooked up to a spring gun. You put the drop in here, regulate the tension of the spring, and firing the gun releases this rod which delivers the drop an appropriate smack." His fingers with their immaculately groomed nails worked deftly. "We don't get a controlled measurement, of course, but it'll show you what I mean. . . . Where do you hide your outlets?"

"Behind the fish tank. Be careful not to disconnect the aerator."

"The screen on that end will show you the energy output. Watch now."

The horizontal green line on the little gray screen bucked at the firing of the spring, then exploded into an oscillating fence of spikes.

"Mad, isn't it?" remarked Dr. Thorne. "Hit it again, but lower the tension of the spring."

If anything, the spikes were even higher.

"The smack-energy ratio isn't proportional," said Seppel. "Sometimes a little nudge will set it off like a rocket. And again, after we tapped it for a week at Ann Arbor figuring out what it was, it showed a tendency to sulk and wouldn't perform at all after awhile."

"The energy output," Thorne said. "It's really quite small, isn't it?"

"Yes, but still surprising for an object this size." He removed the drop from the device and put it back into its little box. "We think that glowing heart has something to do with it. And those gold threads—they are gold, you know—come in there too. Old Camestres, the Medalist himself, was visiting the University, and he says that glow is something that'll have the physicists crawling the walls."

"Oh, come now," said Dr. Thorne broadly.

"You just wait," said Seppel. "We haven't done the analysis yet, but we expect great things. The glow," he added, "isn't hard radiation, if that's what you're thinking."

Willy was proud of it, Thorne thought. It was really his discovery after all, not Thorne's, and Seppel, who found challenge and stimulation in the oddest places, had hit the heights with the little golden drops.

But Thorne was remembering a larger drop, the size of a man's fist, and the charred body of a dead man.

"I found another specimen," he said, turning to a drawer in the worktable. "A larger one." He took out Mr. Zandbergen's drop.

"This is wonderful!" Seppel cried. "It's almost the size of a grapefruit! Now we can—"

Thorne cut him off gently. "I want to tell you about this one. Then I'll turn it over to you. When I first found it, it was irregularly shaped. Lumpy. Ugly. It's smooth now, just like the others, but it changed right before my eyes. It just seemed to run fluid, then coalesce again into the drop shape. And there's something else."

He told Seppel about the attempt to crack the thing and the abrupt heating of the tire iron.

"Yes, that could be," Seppel decided. "It's easily possible that a larger specimen such as this one could cause a metal object near it to become perceptibly warm. Infrared rays aren't hot in themselves, but when they penetrate a material their wave length is increased and the energy released heats the material. In the case of the tire iron, the conductivity of the metal was greater than that of your hand, and you felt the warm iron before the skin itself was affected."

"The iron wasn't warm, Willy. It was damn hot. And in a matter of seconds."

Seppel shook his head. "I don't know what to say. It's the funniest thing I've ever run across."

"The dead man who lay down on it didn't think it was funny," said Thorne.

"You don't think this little thing killed him, do you? He was charred to a cinder all along one side of him. Do you know what kind of infrared could do a thing like that? None."

"I didn't say I thought *this* one killed him," said Thorne, with a cue that Seppel chose to ignore. "I just said the body was right on top of it."

"Too wild for me," said Seppel. He got up, stretched leisurely, and glanced at the clock. "And anyhow, it's sack time. We can worry about it tomorrow, eh?"

Thorne had to smile. Good old Willy. No little glowing monster was going to keep *him* from his sleep.

"We'll put grapefruit back in the drawer," Seppel suggested, "have ourselves a snack, and go to bed."

"Wouldn't the big one be better off in a pail of ice?" asked Thorne, half laughingly.

"If it did decide to give out, it would probably melt the pail before it melted the ice. And besides," he added with dapper complacency, "they never radiate unless they're disturbed."

In the dream, there was sand all around him. He was in it, buried up to his neck. There was a sun overhead that was gold and transparent, and a wind that never seemed to reach his feverish face threw up little whirls of yellow sand.

Sometimes the familiar face of a woman was there. He cried her name and she was gone. And after that, he forgot her, for small shapeless things gamboled out on the sand into the sunlight, only to be burnt black as the rays struck them. . . .

For the fifth time that night, it seemed, Thorne awoke, his eyes staring widely into the darkness. He cursed at himself and turned the perspiration-soaked pillow over, pummeling it into a semblance of plumpness. Seppel lay beside him, snoring gently.

Somewhere in the lodge a timber creaked, and he felt the fear come back again, and saw the black, huddled heap lying before his headlights, and felt the pain renewed in his slowly healing hand. Of the dream, strangely enough, there was no memory at all.

Only the fear.

But why should he be afraid? There was nothing out there. Nothing out there at all.

But the heap in the road. Lightning. *But the little one had burned*. So what? *The little one was too small to burn a man seriously*. I know that. *He was burned*. Lightning, you silly fool! *He was burned!* Shut up. *One of them burned him.* Shut up! Shut up! *There's another one out there tonight.*

No. Nothing out there at all.

Nothing but the dunes and the lake. Nothing.

The wind squalls strummed the pine branches out there, and swirls of sand borne up the bluff from the beach below tickled faintly at the window. The waves of Michigan were roaring out there—but there was nothing else.

Finally, he was able to sleep.

It was nearly dawn when he woke again, but this time he was on guard and alert as he lowered his bare feet softly to the floor. His hand closed over the barrel of a flashlight on the chest of drawers, and he moved noiselessly so that he would not wake the sleeper beside him.

He tiptoed slowly through the workroom and the living room. Something was on the porch.

As he came through the doors, he said sharply: "Who's there?"

An odor of burned wood hit his nostrils. He exclaimed shortly under his breath and shone the light down near the sill of the outside door. There was a round black hole in the door, smoking and glowing faintly around the edges.

He raced back into the workroom and pulled out the drawer that had held the grapefruit-sized drop. It was empty, and a hole gaped in the bottom of it. The hard wood was still burning slowly.

He yanked out the drawer, put it in the kitchen sink, and turned on the water. Then he filled a pan and soaked the hole in the door thoroughly.

They never radiate unless they're disturbed! That was a laugh. Not only had it radiated, but it had somehow focused the radiation. Dr. Thorne was no physicist, but he began to wonder whether the meter had told the whole story of the little glowing drop.

He unlocked the door and slid out into the night. Below the stair was a small, almost imperceptible track in the sand. He followed it down the ridge of the dune, lost it momentarily in a patch of scrub, then found it again in the undisturbed expanse of the sand blow.

He went down into the silent valley, the bobbling yellow light from his flash throwing the tiny track into high relief.

When he reached the center of the bowl, he stopped among the long shadows of the gaunt spiky trees.

There was another track in the sand, meeting and merging with the little one. And the track was three feet wide.

He followed it as if in a dream to the crest of the first low shore dune and stood on its summit among the sharp grass and wild grape. The moon's crescent was low over the water and orange. He saw the track go down the slope and disappear into the waves which were swirling in a new depression in the sand.

The wind whipped his pajama shirt about his back as he stood there and knew that he was afraid of that track in the sand, and that no lightning had killed the little tramp.

It was not until he had locked the door of the lodge behind him that he realized he had run all of the way back.

Friday was a quiet day in the dunes country, but the police did receive three minor complaints. A farmer charged that someone had not only made off with and eaten three of his best laying hens, but had burned the feathers and bones and left them right in the chicken yard. The Ottawa County Highway Commission wanted to know who was building fires in the middle of their asphalt roads and plastering the landscape with hot tar. And a maiden lady complained that the artists in the local summer colony must be holding Wild Orgies again from the looks of the lights she had seen over there at three A.M.

Dr. Thorne bent down over the tracks in the sand. It certainly looked to him as though the big one had been waiting for Mr. Zandbergen's drop.

Seppel said, "Get out of the way there," and snapped his Graflex. "These sand tracks won't last long in the winds around here. And I frankly tell you that if I hadn't seen it with my own eyes, I would never have believed it." He circled the point of conjunction, laid his fountain pen beside it for size reference, and the Graflex flashed again.

"We'll want the door, too," he said, putting the camera aside and scrawling in his notebook.

Thorne howled.

"Well, just the part with the hole in it then," Seppel conceded. "Did you find out where the large track came from?"

"I tracked it to the woods. The ground there is too soft and boggy to hold a wide track like that, and I finally lost it."

Seppel struggled to his feet and retrieved his coat, which he had hung for safety's sake on the white peg branch of a skeleton tree. "Just imagine the size of an object which would make a three-foot track in soft sand!" he exclaimed. "And to think it's been in the lake for heaven knows how long and this is the first time it's come into evidence!"

"I wouldn't be too sure about that—about this being the first time, I mean. There have been some funny old stories told along these shores. I heard one myself from my grandmother when I was about twelve. About the dune roller that was bigger than a schooner and lived in the caves at the bottom of the lake. It came out every hundred years and rolled through the dune forest, leaving a strip of bare sand behind it where it had eaten the vegetation. They said it looked for a man, and when it found one, it would stop rolling and sink back into the lake."

"Great Caesar," said Seppel solemnly. "I can see it now—the great glowing globe lurking deep in the caverns where the sun never shines and there is no life except a few diatoms drifting in the motionless waters."

Thorne gaped at his friend for a minute, and then spied a suspicious twinkle in one blue eye.

"This is no laughing matter, you Sunday supplementist!" he said sharply.

"Hmp," said Willy Seppel, and brushed a few grains of sand from the sleeve of his handsome suit.

It was late when Miss Jeanne Wright got out of the movie in Muskegon—so late that she barely had time to do the shopping which had, ostensibly, been her reason for taking *Carlin* out. "You just can't buy decent dresses in Port Grand, Uncle Kirk," she had pleaded, and he really wouldn't mind if she took the boat, would he? MacInnes had growled indulgently from the depths of his new pan-adaptor and said he certainly did, confound it, and what was the matter with using the car? But he had tossed her the keys just the same.

The street lights of the city were going on when, laden with bundles, she finally hailed a cab and drove to the yacht basin. It was a beautiful evening, with soft-glowing stars in a sky that was still red-purple in the west. *Carlin* slipped majestically out among the anchored craft into Muskegon Lake.

A bonfire blazed cheerfully on the shore and singing voices from some beach party floated melodiously out over the water. They shouted a jocular greeting to *Carlin* and Jeanne blew a hail to them with the air horn. Her heart was light as she led the cruiser through the channel into the lake and headed for home.

A secretive smile danced on her lips, and she thought kindly about a certain stern-faced young biologist. He was a strange man, occasionally even rude in an unintentional sort of way, and preoccupied with such dreary things as plant cycles and environmental adaptations. But he had walked with her in the dunes one day and changed for a little while, and kissed her once, very gently, on the lips. And after that she had known what she wanted.

He would be sitting in his workroom now, looking over the day's bugs and not thinking of her at all. Or perhaps he would be talking to her uncle over the radio.

She hummed dreamily to herself. The cruiser's speed increased to twenty, and it rocked momentarily in a trough, setting the little good luck charm hung up over the wheel to bobbing like a pendulum. Ian had given that to her. She loved it because of that.

After a while she turned on the short wave receiver that sat on one of the lockers in the deckhouse and listened to Ian and her uncle.

"I have a colleague of mine out from Ann Arbor," Thorne was saying. "About that amber drop we found. Remember my telling you about it? I gave one to Jeanne for a souvenir. My friend is a biophysicist and thinks the drops are a great scientific discovery. His name is Willy Seppel. Say something, Willy."

"Gambusia," said Seppel, recalling the minnows in the larvae pail.

Jeanne listened absently. Ian was telling how the drops gave off hot light when they were disturbed. How he thought there might be bigger drops around that could really grind out the energy 40db. above S9 (What in the world did *that* mean?) Thorne and this Willy person would look for the bigger drops.

"Is it really hot?" Jeanne wondered, staring curiously at

the pendant drop, swinging above the binnacle in its miniature silver basket. It didn't seem to be. But then Ian had said the little ones didn't radiate very much. Only enough to tickle a something-or-other.

Far out in the lake, the lights of an ore boat twinkled. She passed the little village of Lake Harbor and put out a bit farther from shore. There would be no more towns now until Port Grand.

Over the radio, her Uncle Kirk's voice, homely and kind, was describing the great things in store for the new panadaptor. Ian would put in a comment here and there, but she noticed that he sounded tired, poor darling.

Cleanly, powerfully, *Carlin* sliced through the waves, pursuing the shadow of herself. The shadow was long, and very black. A boat with a searchlight, thought Jeanne, and looked astern.

It was there, riding high in the dark, choppy water: a great glowing globe of phosphorescence not twenty yards off the stern. It was coming after her, rapidly overtaking the cruiser.

She screamed then, and when the thing came on, she opened the throttle and attempted to outmaneuver it. But the great glowing monster would pause while she veered and spiraled, then overtake her easily when she tried to run away. The motors of the Matthews throbbed in the hull beneath her feet as she tried to urge them to a speed they were never meant for.

The thing was drawing closer. She could see trails of water streaming from it. What was it? What would it do if it caught her?

Bigger ones! Her eyes turned with horror to the tiny drop on its silver chain. Its glow was the perfect minature of the monstrous thing in the water behind her. She sobbed as she wrenched *Carlin's* wheel from side to side in hysterical frenzy. Across the cabin, the quiet voice of Ian was telling MacInnes how to rig the panadaptor as a frequency monitor.

Ian!

And if you're ever in a jam. . . .

With tears streaming down her cheeks she set the automatic pilot and fumbled with the little amateur transmitter that had been built into the locker. She had seen her uncle use it only once. That turned it on, she thought, but how did she know it was set right? Or did you set these things?

The little panel wore three switches, two knobs, a dial and a little red light. Naturally Kirk MacInnes had not labeled the controls of an instrument he had built himself. The panel was innocent of any such clutterment.

Carlin tore through the night. The glowing thing was less than fifteen yards behind.

Jeanne wept wildly and the placid voices over the receiver spoke sympathetically of the ruining of Thorne's beach pool by the storm.

Oh, those knobs and switches! This one, then this one, she thought. No—that wouldn't be right. The transmitter might not even be on the air at all. Or she might be in some part of the band where Ian and her uncle would fail to hear her. But what was she supposed to do? And she couldn't read this funny tuning scale.

"I've got a swell mobile VFO in *Carlin,*" said MacInnes.

"What's VFO?" said Seppel.

"In Mac's case, it means Very Frequently Offband."

Laughter.

Oh, what difference would it make? What could he do to help her? The brilliance of the huge thing was lighting up the water for yards around.

The calm voices floated from the receiver and the globe drew closer than it had ever been.

She clawed at the stand-by switch of the radio and suddenly her sobs and the beat of the engines were the only sounds in the deckhouse. She would try. That was all. She would try to reach Ian, and pray that her uncle had left the transmitter set to the correct frequency.

"Ian!" she cried, then remembered to press the button on the side of the little hand microphone. Forcing back her tears, she said, "Ian, Ian—can you hear me?"

Trembling, her hand touched the receiver.

"Jeanne!" the sound burst into the deckhouse. "Is that you? What are you doing?"

"It's after me, Ian!" she screamed. "A glowing sphere fifteen feet high! It's chasing the boat!"

"The boat," came MacInnes' voice numbly. "She took it to Muskegon."

"Jeanne! Listen to me. I don't know whether this will do any good, but you must try. You must do exactly as I say. Do you hear me?"

"I hear you. Ian! That thing is almost on top of the boat!"

"Listen. Listen to me, darling. You have that little amber drop somewhere in the boat. Do you remember? The little amber drop I gave you. Get it. Take it and throw it overboard. Throw it as far as you can. The amber drop! Now tell me if you heard me."

"Yes. I hear you. The drop. . . ."

The drop. It danced on its little silver chain and the light in its core was bright and pulsating and warm. She tore it from its place over the wheel and groped back to the open cockpit of the cruiser. She clung for a full minute to the canopy stanchion, blinded by the golden light.

And then the small drop arched brightly over the water, even as a meteor had, many centuries past.

The light, reflecting off the walls painted a flat, clinical white, was full of blurred, fuzzy forms. They might have been almost anything, Thorne thought. And he shuddered as he thought of what they might have been. A table, for instance, with a burden that was sprawled and made black all along one side.

Without moving his head or changing his expression he squeezed his eyes shut very slowly and opened them again. But it was not the medical examiner's office. It was the waiting room of the little local hospital, and Willy Seppel was sitting beside him on the leather couch. Through the open window behind lowered blinds, a clovery night breeze stirred, parting the smoke that filled the room and turning a page of the magazine that Seppel was staring at.

A young man of twenty-five or so sat across the room from them and ate prodigious quantities of Lifesavers. "My wife," he had grinned nervously at them. "Our first."

The persons in the waiting room could see through the open door to a room at the end of the hall. People in white would periodically enter and leave this room, but another, grimmer group which had entered nearly an hour ago had not come out.

"Willy, I'm going nuts," Thorne burst out at last. "What are they doing in there? You'd think they'd at least let me know—let me see her."

"Easy. It'll be any minute now." He proffered a gold cigarette case, but Thorne shook his head. "Why don't you lie back and try to relax?" Seppel said. "You've been crouching there staring at the floor until your eyes look like a pair of burned-out bulbs. What good do you think you're going to do her in that kind of shape?"

Thorne sank back and lay with the back of his hand shading his eyes. If he could have been there when they brought her in! But it takes time to find where an unmanned boat has drifted. Time while he sat before his receiver with nothing to do but wait. The hands of the clock had wound around to one A.M. before the call finally came and he knew she was saved.

It was three-thirty now. MacInnes and his wife were in there with her. He looked despairingly down the white corridor, and waited.

The sound of her voice, made broken and breathless with weeping, rose again in his mind. She had said the thing was fifteen feet high. The big one itself. And it could have—

This wouldn't do at all. The memory of his dream the previous night stood out in his mind with horrible clarity. The bright golden sun and the little burned things. But infrared doesn't burn. The bright golden sun.

"Sun," said Dr. Thorne to himself, very quietly.

"Mm'mm?" said Seppel.

"Sun," he repeated firmly. "Willy, do you always think the same way?"

"Nope."

"If I hit you, how do you think?"

"Mad," said Seppel, with a winning smile.

"But if you figure the best way to sneak out of here without being seen, how do you think?"

"Rationally."

"I've been thinking about the drops again. You know, we've got a pretty serious discrepancy in the so-called properties of the things. We've proved the infrared emission, but infrared doesn't sear flesh."

"That's what I've been trying to tell you," said Seppel, with patience.

"Nonetheless, I'm convinced that the big one Jeanne saw is the thing that did in the tramp. Now what if the energy emitted is not always infrared? What if the infrared is a sort of involuntary result of the blows we gave the drop, while ordinarily when it's aroused it gives off another wave length? Say something in the visible with a lot of energy, that that drop shape could focus into a beam."

Seppel didn't say a thing.

Silence precipitated heavily. The young man in the chair opposite them shifted his position and stared at them with gaping awe. Scientists!

There was a starchy swish and a nurse appeared in the doorway. Thorne started to his feet. "Can we—"

"Mr. De Angelo," she beckoned coolly. "It's a boy. Will you follow me, please?"

The young man gave a joyous, inarticulate cry and rushed out of the room.

Thorne dropped back. "Ye gods," he muttered.

"You've really got it bad, haven't you?" Seppel marveled.

"Oh, Willy, shut up. You know I'm only interested in her because of the thing that chased her. And wipe that look off your face. Between you and MacInnes a man doesn't have a chance."

Seppel looked slightly hurt.

"I'm sorry," Thorne apologized briefly. He walked around the room. The young man with the new son had been so anxious to leave that he had forgotten his Lifesavers. Thorne ate one. It was wintergreen. He hated wintergreen.

Sepple yawned delicately, then leaned forward and glanced out the door. "Someone's coming," he warned softly.

A tall man in a uniform of summer tans had left the room at the end of the corridor and walked purposefully toward the waiting room.

Seppel rose to his feet as the man entered the room. He said: "Good evening—or rather, good morning. Is there something I can do?"

"My name is Cunningham, commander of the Coast Guard cutter *Manistique*. Are you Mr. Ian Thorne?"

"My name is Seppel. This is Mr. Thorne. Won't you sit down?"

"Thanks, I will." To Thorne, who stood with his hands rudely clasped behind his back, he said briskly: "Mr. Thorne, at nine this evening your amateur station contacted our base with information that the cruiser *Carlin* was in difficulty off the mainland somewhere between Port Grand and Muskegon."

"It wasn't me, it was Kirk MacInnes." Thorne was not interested in brisk, nautical gentlemen.

"We found the cruiser drifting, out of gas, some seven miles off the Port Grand light. Miss Wright, the operator of the craft, was found lying unconscious on the cockpit floor. I've just seen her—"

"How is she?" Thorne cut in.

"The doctors say she is suffering from shock, but other than that, they can't find a thing wrong with her. Now what I'd like to know—"

"Is she conscious? Has she been able to talk?"

"She's very weak and what she says makes no sense. I thought perhaps you might be able to help us on that score."

Thorne looked at the Coast-Guardsman narrowly. "We were conversing with her over the radio, when she suddenly seemed to become disturbed and evidently fainted."

"Didn't MacInnes tell you anything?" asked Seppel.

"No."

"Quiet, Willy," Thorne said.

"She seemed to be trying to tell us that someone was chasing her," Cunningham persisted. "Are you sure she said nothing in her talk with you that could give us a hint of the trouble?"

"I knew there was something wrong from the sound of her voice. That's all. When she didn't answer, Mr. MacInnes radioed the Coast Guard."

"And we found her after a four-hour search. That young lady was very lucky that she ran out of gas. Her automatic pilot had the cruiser headed straight out into the middle of the lake."

"There was—nothing else on the water near her?"

"The lake was empty." Cunningham paused, then said casually, "Was there something you expected us to find, Dr. Thorne?"

"Certainly not. I was just wondering."

"I see." The officer got to his feet. "I don't mind telling you gentlemen that I think there's something you're not letting me know. My job is done, and it's true that legally I have no business questioning you at all. But my business *is*

keeping the waterways safe. The young lady in the roon
down the hall didn't faint from nervous exhaustion o
hunger. Something scared the hell out of her out there o
the lake. If you know what it was, I wish you'd tell me!"

"Have you ever read any science fiction, Commande
Cunningham?" Seppel asked, toying with his gold cigarett
case. Rather belatedly, he said, "Cigarette?"

The Coast-Guardsman took one with suspicious thanks
"Are you trying to tell me that the little green Martian
have put outboards on their rocket ships and are chasin
the pleasure craft on our lake?"

Thorne said harshly: "What Dr. Seppel means is this
We have reason to believe that a highly unusual occurrenc
was responsible for tonight's unpleasantness. I don't like t
mince words, Commander. I think I *do* know what was ou
there last night, but I'm not going to tell you. I can't begi
to prove my suspicions, and I have a rather intense aver-
sion to being laughed at."

"I have no intention of laughing, Mr. Thorne. But if yo
have information relative to marine safety, let me remin
you that you have an obligation to report it to the prope
authorities."

"Proper authorities are not notorious for their sympathy
They'd laugh in my face. No, thank you, Commander. Until I have proof, I say nothing."

The door at the end of the corridor opened once more
and closed softly. Kirk MacInnes and his wife came dow
toward the waiting room. Thorne started up.

"She wants to see you, son," MacInnes said tiredly
"She's a little stronger now, and she asked for you. I'm taking Ellen back home. This has been pretty raw for her."

"I'm all right," his wife said stiffly. She clutched a damp
tightly balled lace handkerchief, but her features were im-
mobile.

"Will Jeanne be all right?" Thorne asked brokenly.

"She'll be fine," said MacInnes, clapping him on th
back. "Now get down there and see her before those
medics decide she can't have any more visitors."

"I'm there now. And—thanks, Mac." He disappeared
down the corridor. The engineer and his wife left quietly.

"Thorne is a good man," Seppel said, "even if he is a
trifle mule-headed." His bright blue eyes looked humorous-
ly into the half-angry face of the Coast Guard officer. He

laughed, moved over on the leather couch, and said: "Sit down here, Commander. Have another cigarette. Have a Lifesaver. I'm going to tell you a singular story."

It was shortly before lunchtime in Thorne's dune lodge, but the bubbling beaker on the range that Willy Seppel was stirring exuded a decidedly unappetizing aroma. Pungent, acidic in an organic kind of way, with noisome and revolting overtones, the fumes finally brought indignant remarks from Thorne.

"Look," he said, peering in the doorway, and holding his nose. "I'm the last one to criticize another man's cooking, but will you tell me what in heaven's name that is?"

"Oh, just a bit of digestive juice," said Seppel cheerily, turning off the gas and removing the beaker with a pair of pot holders. He carried his foul-steaming container into the workroom. Thorne fled before him.

"I suppose I'd better not ask where you got it," he said, from the sanctuary of the radio room.

"Don't be silly," said Seppel. "I merely raided your enzymes and warmed up a batch. Just an idea."

He took the little drop out of its container and set it on the table beside the beaker. "I thought since digestive juice provoked it into emitting once, it might do it again."

Thorne regarded him dubiously.

"I only wish," Seppel went on to say, "that the grapefruit-sized one hadn't escaped." He set the drop in a loop of plastic and dipped it into the brew.

"Take it easy with that one, Willy. It's the only link we have with the big one."

"So you think they can communicate, too," said Seppel without looking up.

"I don't know whether it's communication or sympathetic vibration or the call of the wild. But that thing did follow Jeanne because of the little drop in the boat, and it disappeared when it got what it wanted. The grapefruit heard mama, too, and got away. I'll bet if that little one had been strong enough to get through your fancy insulation, it would have disappeared along with the other one."

"And the two tracks merged into one," said Seppel, testing the soaked drop in the thermocouple. Nothing happened. "As the rustic detective was heard to remark, 'They was two sets o' footsteps leadin' to the scene of the crime, and only one set leadin' away.' I wonder what kind of a molecular bond that transparent envelope has?" He felt the drop with his finger, shrugged, and put it back into the juice.

"The big globe killed the tramp, if my idea is correct," said Thorne. "He must have seen the thing coming out of the lake, turned to beat it, and fell on his face. And I think he picked exactly the wrong place to fall."

"On grapefruit," Seppel agreed. "All mama wanted to do was to pick up her offspring. She couldn't help it if there was a body in the way."

"But she killed just the same," said Thorne. "Those old dune roller stories hint that she may have done it before." He fished the miniature drop out of the liquid and looked into its yellow heart meditatively.

"And Willy," he said abstractedly, "unless something is done soon, she'll do it again."

During the days that followed, Dr. Thorne went about his work with quiet preoccupation; and this in itself was enough to make Seppel more than a little suspicious. He rarely mentioned the drops, although he visited Jeanne every day, carrying sheaves of flowers and boxes of candy and fruit. Seppel went along on these pilgrimages for the ride, but almost always tactfully declined visiting the sickroom and hiked out instead to the Coast Guard station for a parley with his new ally, Commander Cunningham.

Anxiety furrowed Seppel's pink forehead as he paced up and down the officer's quarters. "He's got something up his sleeve," he maintained. "He goes off in the jeep in the morning and doesn't come back until noon. When I ask him where he's been, he says he just went into town to see Jeanne. But visiting hours are from two to four! If he doesn't go to the hospital, where does he go?"

Cunningham shrugged, and picked up a folded newspaper that lay on the table. "Have you seen this, Willy? It might explain a few things."

Mystified, Seppel read aloud: " 'We pay CASH for certain unusual minerals. Highest prices, free pickup. Samples wanted are round, semi-transparent, amber colored with metallic veining. HURRY! Write today, Box 236, Port Grand, Michigan.' "

Seppel stared aghast.

"I take it you weren't acquainted with this," the officer said. He walked to the window and looked down at a fruiter steaming through the channel. "Do you know what he plans to do?"

"No, but I know what I'd do. There's some kind of an attraction between the big globe and the drops—a force that draws the little ones home to mama when they get her call. We found that out with a drop at Thorne's lodge. But that attraction is so great that it works the other way too. Little Miss Wright told you that. If the drops can't come, if we hold them back, mama comes after her children. That's what Thorne will probably count on."

It was Cunningham's turn to stare. "You mean he'll use the drops from the ad for *bait?*"

Seppel said gently: "What's a man to do, Rob? He can't let it go free. The fellow that finds the monster has three choices: he can run home and hide under the bed, and pretend he didn't see it at all, he can try to inform the proper authorities, or he can attempt to dispose of the monster himself. Thorne knows nobody will believe his dune roller story so he just doesn't waste time convincing people."

Cunningham turned abruptly from the window and said violently: "You aren't going to start on me too, are you, Willy? Sure. Here I am, one slightly used but still serviceable authority. I believe your damn dune roller yarn for some reason or other. But it doesn't do any good. I'd earn the biggest haw-haw from here to the Straits of Mackinac if I tried to initiate an official search for a round glowing thing fifteen feet high. The world won't unite simply because Michigan has itself a monster, you know. And what can I do, even if I take the *Manistique* out? Maybe Ian Thorne knows how to catch monsters, but I certainly don't."

"You want to let him go on, I suppose," Seppel said. He added a trifle wistfully, "I hate to see him get his hide fried off when he's just beginning to think about settling down."

"You watch him. That's all. And let me know when you think he's going to pull something. I'll do everything I can." He glanced at his watch. "I have to get out of here now, Willy. Keep your eyes open. All *we* can do is wait."

"And that," said Seppel, with dark doubt shading his pleasant voice, "seems to be all there is to say."

The drops glowed on the kitchen table. "Seven!" said Ian Thorne triumphantly. "How do they look to you, Willy? From the size of a pea to a tennis ball. Seven little devil eyes."

"What are you going to do with them?" asked Seppel. He wore an old lab apron over his trousers and wiped the breakfast dishes. It was very early in the morning.

"Just a little experiment. I got a bright idea the other day while I was visiting Jeanne. You can have the drops after I'm finished if you like, but I want to try this thing out first."

"I wish you'd let me help you."

"No, Willy."

"Cunningham believes you, too," Seppel went on recklessly. "Why don't you tell us what you're going to do?"

"No." He scooped the drops into a bakelite box. "I'll be gone most of the day. I have some collecting to do out in the dunes."

He vanished into the bedroom and came out wearing hiking boots and a heavy leather jacket. An empty knapsack dangled over his arm. He put the bakelite box into the buckled pouch on the outside of the sack, and took a paper packet from the sink and stuffed it into his back pocket.

"Oops! Almost forgot my collecting bottles," he laughed, and went into the radio room.

Seppel put down the dish towel and stepped softly after him. There were no collecting bottles in the radio room. He was just in time to see Thorne drop a handful of little metal cylinders and a black six-inch gadget into the knapsack.

Thorne did not seem at all abashed to find Seppel standing there. He brushed past and went out the kitchen door.

"So long, Willy. Keep the home fires burning. Send out the posse if I'm not back before dark." The screen door slammed.

After waiting a minute, Seppel grabbed up the binoculars from the china shelf and glided silently through the sandy yard, past the generator building to the path that led down the side of the dune to the shed where the jeep was kept.

The early morning mist still curled around the trees and

settled in the hollows, and a distant bird call echoed down on the forest floor. At a bend in the steep path, Seppel caught a glimpse of Thorne's broad back dappled by the pale sun rising through the fog.

The path turned sharply and cut off diagonally down the dune toward the shed. Instead of continuing, Seppel stepped off the path, and treading cautiously, circled across through the woods to arrive at a point on the slope directly above the garage. Then he removed his apron, spread it on the twiggy, dew-wet ground, and stretched out among the bushes, bringing his binoculars to bear on the man below.

Thorne removed a small wooden crate from the rear of the jeep. It bore the red-stenciled inscription:

G. B. VANDER VREES & SONS—HIGHWAY CONSTRUCTION

There were other words, too, but Thorne stood in the way of Seppel's vision. He quickly transferred the contents of the crate to his knapsack, and with a single look around him, set off down the dune trail that ran through the forest, parallel to the lake shore.

As soon as Thorne was out of sight, Willy Seppel scrambled heavily to his feet and went back up the path to the lodge. There he addressed some intense words to the microphone of the amateur station, an operation which would have been frowned upon by the FCC, which discourages the use of such equipment by unlicensed persons.

He would have maintained his disinterest and scientific detachment if he had been asked about it, but the truth was that Dr. Ian Thorne deeply loved the dunes. He had lived in them during his childhood, grown up and gone away, and come back to find them substantially the same. He recalled that had surprised him a little. You expected the dunes to change, they were like a person, though only one who has known the heights and swamps of them can explain the curious sleeping vitality of the sands under the forest. Things with a smaller life than the dunes would flutter and creep and stalk boldly through them until you might think of them as dead and tame. But Dr. Thorne had seen the traveling dunes shifting restlessly before the winds and felt a kinship with the great never-lasting hills.

The path he strolled along was an old friend. He had

pursued the invertebrate citizens of the forest along its meandering length, waded in the marshy inter-dunal pools which it carefully skirted, and had itched from encounters with the poison ivy that festooned the trunks and shrubs beside it.

The path wound along the shore for a good five miles—horizontally, at least—and he did not hurry. The knapsack was too heavy, for one thing, and the still air was warming slowly as the sun rose up through the pines and oak trees. An insect chirred sleepily in a gorge on his right, and as if at some prearranged signal, an excursion of mosquitoes bobbed out to worry the back of his neck.

The path took him through a clearing in the sand covered with patches of dusty, green grass and scarlet Indian weed. On the lee side of a great bare dune at the edge of the clearing stood a single, short cottonwood, half buried in the sand. But the tree had grown upward to escape, modifying its lower branches into roots. The tree was one of the few forms of life that defied the dunes—by growing with them—and its branches were brave and green.

Thoughtfully, Thorne passed on again into the dimmer depths of the forest.

It was nearly noon when he reached the foot of a cluster of sand dunes, the principal peak of which rose some hundred and fifty feet above the floor of the woods. It was the highest point for many miles along the shore, and its name was Mount Scott. The path circled its eastern slope and then continued on, but Thorne stepped off onto the faintly defined, spider-web laced trail leading to the summit.

The going was rough. Thornapple branches probed after his eyes, and as the ascent grew steeper, sudden shifts in the dirty sand under his feet brought him to his knees. The tree roots across the path had partially blocked the sand, forming crude natural steps in the lower reaches of the dune; but as he climbed higher, the trees were left behind while the sand grew cleaner and hotter, and the wild grape, creeper and ubiquitous poison ivy became the prevalent greenery.

He was winded and perspiring when he finally stood on the peak of the dune. He glanced briefly about him and selected a spot partially shaded by a scrub juniper as his campsite. He sat down, shucked the knapsack and his heavy jacket, and lit a cigarette.

The hills below rolled away in gentle, green waves toward the farmlands and orchards in the east and the brilliant blue lake in the west. He could see the spires of the town of Port Grand poking out of the haze a few miles down the shore, and some white sails appeared off the promontory that hid the entrance to the river harbor.

He turned his attention to Mount Scott itself. The summit of the dune was really composed of two shallow humps, with a depression on the lakeward side in which Thorne had made his camp. Below this, a sheer, fairly clean slope of sand swept down to the low tangle of woods which lay between him and the shore.

He looked cautiously in the knapsack and removed the seven small drops, grouping them in a circle on the white sand of the lake slope. After that, he retreated to his hollow and settled down as comfortably as he could.

The paper packet in his pocket yielded three ham-and-pickle sandwiches, slightly soggy, which he consumed leisurely. A short foray around the peak brought dessert in the form of a handful of late blueberries. After his meal he employed himself at length with the contents of the knapsack. When the job was finally done, he sat down under the juniper tree and began to wait.

The shade of the tree diminished, disappeared as the sun climbed higher, and then reappeared on the other side of the tree, leaving Thorne with the sun in his face and a monumental thirst. The blueberries, unfortunately, were all gone.

At last, at four P.M., the largest drop began to move.

It rolled slowly out of the shallow hole in the sand that cupped it and moved down the hill. Thorne watched it roll *up* a small pile of sand that blocked its path and disappear into the woods at the foot of the hill.

At 4:57 one of the smaller drops followed in the track of the first. It had a little trouble when it came to the pile of sand—which was one of several strung across the face of the dune—but it negotiated the obstacle at last and disappeared.

Just as the sun was beginning to redden the water, the third drop began its descent. Quietly, Thorne rose and replaced it in its hole. The faint gleam within it might have grown a bit brighter when he interfered, but perhaps it was only the reflection of the sun.

The five remaining drops were grouped in a horseshoe, downward pointing, and the drop whose elopement had just been foiled reposed at the end of one prong. A few minutes later, the larger drop at the other prong attempted to roll down the hill. Thorne put it back and rapped sharply on each of the others with his cigarette lighter, tamping them down further into the sand. He was strained forward alertly now, with his eyes on the strip of forest below. The sun slipped grudgingly behind the flat lake, and a tang of pine washed up the slope. The drops did not move again.

With the departure of the sun, the glow in the heart of each alien thing leaped higher and higher, until the string of them was like a softly glowing corona in the sand—a strange earthbound constellation.

But their glow was not beauty, Thorne reminded himself. It was death. Death had dwelt in their great, glowing mother who had already called two of her incredible children home. Death that rolled seeking through the lake and the dune forest. . . .

His cigarette end made a dimmer eye in the dusk than the glow of the drops. There was still enough light to see by—the sky was red around him and the dune forest was silent.

He wondered idly what long forgotten power had strewn the drops along the shore. They were not terrestial, he was almost sure of that. Perhaps they had been a meteor that had exploded over the lake, and the life of the great thing —if it was life—had been patiently gathering up its scattered substance ever since, assimilating the fragments during its long rests at the bottom of the lake.

From the size of it, it must have been growing for hundreds of years, collecting a drop of itself here and there, from roadbeds and sand dunes and farmyards, responding to those who imprudently hindered it with the only defense it knew.

And now he was to destroy it. It had killed a man. Perhaps before this, even, men had found the drops attractive and carelessly put them in their pockets . . . and the dune roller sought a man. It had killed the little tramp, and almost killed Jeanne. He couldn't take a chance of letting it go again.

The image of Jeanne rose in his mind. The memory of the time they had walked down the winding forest path, and of a twig caught in her sandal. She had had grains of sand on her tanned arms, and a bright yellow flower stuck crazily in one dark curl. She had laughed when he plumped her down on the moss-soft root of an old oak and took the twig out, but she had not laughed when he kissed her.

Around him, the forest was still.

A cold breath whispered along his skin. The forest was still. Not a bird, not an insect, not an animal noise. The forest was still.

He felt like yelling at it: *Come on out, you!* Come out and chase me like you chased her!

He fingered the stud of the little black instrument in his hand. He would show it. Let it dare to come out.

Come out!

It came.

He had never dreamed it would be so big.

It had made no noise at all. In a fascination of horror he watched it roll to the foot of the tall dune. It vanished among the trees, but a warm yellow radiance lit the undersides of the fluttering leaves as it moved beneath them. The light blazed as it emerged from the brush and came straight toward him, rolling up the hill.

The small drops pulsed in their sandy snares and he gave each one a savage rap. As if it, too, shared the insult, the great globe flared, then subsided sullenly. But its ponderous ascent was alarmingly rapid.

He could not take his eyes away from it. The smaller drops were rocks, were mere bits of oddly glowing crystal; but this great thing before him seemed the most beautiful and the most terrible thing he had ever seen in his life. And it was alive. No man could have looked upon it and said that it was not alive. The brilliant golden heart in it swelled and blazed upon the golden veining that closed it in.

There were noises now from the winding path in the forest below, and the twinkling pinpoint lights of men. But Thorne did not hear them, nor see any light except the great one before him. He could not move. Sweat stood out on his face and the instinct to flee dissolved into terror that folded his legs like boneless things. He half-crouched on hands and knees and stared . . . and stared.

The thing was closer now, nearly up to the line of sand humps that Thorne had worked so hard on. He had to get away. There was no more time. He forced his paralyzed hands and feet to tear into the loose sand of the side of the depression and pull him up. He had to get on the other side of the hill.

In the last instant, his numbed fingers pressed the stud of the little transmitter that would activate the firing caps of the neonitro buried in the sand.

But the monster must have realized, somehow. Because he felt—when he flung himself out over the peak with the deep red sky around him—a searing, mounting pain that started on the inside and flooded outward. He rolled unconscious over the far side of the hill just as the five solemn detonations blasted the golden glowing globe to bits.

There were white, gauzy circles around the place where his eyes looked out. He was vaguely surprised to see six people with the eyes—three sets of two. He made the eyes blink and the six people changed into Seppel, MacInnes and Jeanne. He tried to raise an arm and was rewarded by a fierce jab of pain. The arm was thick and bandaged, like the rest of him.

The six—three—people had seen his eyes open and they moved closer to him. Jeanne sat down beside the bed and leaned her head close.

"I hope that's you in there," she said, and he was amazed to see there were tears in her eyes.

"How am I?" he mumbled through the bandages.

"Medium rare," said Seppel. "You doggone crazy fool."

"We almost got to the top, anyway," said MacInnes gruffly. "But you went and beat us to it."

"Had to," Thorne said painfully.

"You would," Jeanne said.

"Is it gone?" he asked. There were six people again and he felt very tired.

"Shivered to atoms," said Seppel with finality. "You should see the crater in the sand. But we'll still have small ones to study. Your ad brought in four more today. I was talking to Camestres on the phone, and he says he's sure he can swing a nice fat research grant for us as soon as you're able to get out of that bed—"

Thorne groaned.

"He says," Jeanne translated firmly, "that he's sticking to *Ecological Studies of the Michigan Dunes,* Chapter Eight. No more dune rollers, thank you."

MacInnes laughed and wagged his gray old head. "You'd better surrender, Dr. Seppel. Jeanne's got her mind made up. And one thing about her—whatever she says, she'll always be Wright."

"Don't be too sure about that," she said pertly, laying her two small hands gently on Thorne's bandaged arm. It didn't hurt a bit.

High on a dune above the lake, the moon rode high over a blackened crater in the sand. Two of the grains of sand, which gleamed in the moonlight a bit more golden than the rest, tumbled down together into a sheltered hollow to begin anew the work of three hundred years.

No Bath For the Browns

MARGOT BENNET

Before the real estate agent had time to shut his eyes and stick a pin into the waiting list, he found he had rented the house to Mrs. Brown. She took it, unseen, on a ten years' lease, and on her way back to the basement room she and her husband now lived in, she dropped a pound in a pavement artist's hat. The pound marked, for her, the end of a year's exercise in concealing furious despair behind a façade of untroubled, almost aristocratic, courtesy. Now, at last, she had found a house.

When she unlocked the front door she felt like Robinson Crusoe surveying, for the first time, what was to be his kingdom. The grim mosaic of the hall floor would have been naked to the sunshine if it had not been for the porch, a kind of sun baffle-wall in coarsely stained glass. The floor of the porch was also tiled, making it suitable for potted plants.

"A dear little house," Charles said to her, with just a hint of a question in his voice.

Her mind was wandering on. "If we bought a carpet—secondhand, of course—we could cover those tiles."

"And how are we to conceal the railway line which passes under the bedroom window?" Charles asked.

She opened a buff-colored door and peered down the stairs. "Charles," she said in excitement. "There's a bath!"

They looked at the bath. "It isn't very handy." she admitted.

"No," Charles said. "But I suppose you can dive in from the top step and dry in the hall when you come out."

Greta ran upstairs. "Look!" she called. "Here's a room that isn't really good for anything. Don't you think we could move the bath up to this floor?"

"We'd never get anyone to do it inside of six months."

"Nonsense!" she said briskly. "We can do it ourselves.

Cut off the water, move the bath, phone the water and the gas company and say our bath's been connected. Then we'd be priority. We can do it with ropes."

"I begin to see why this house was to let," Charles said.

Greta said she'd meant to tell him about that. It belonged, she said, to a man called Smith whose wife had left him for another man, at least that was what the neighbors said; anyway, she'd disappeared, and he was so heartbroken, the neighbors said, that he couldn't bear to live there any more.

"I'm surprised he ever bore it. Do you think it has a queerish smell?"

"It's probably only rats," Greta said, with a flash of her old spirit. "Now, I'll begin to scrub the floors tomorrow. We must buy some paint for those awful walls. You must get in touch with the storage people and the gas and electricity and water. There's the food office, and we must find a coal merchant who'll have us. Do you think we can get that broken window mended? Do try and eat well through the day—there'll be nothing but bread and margarine in the evenings. And buy some rat poison."

Their lives for the next month might have been planned by some lunatic master mind. One part of the day was spent in making pathetic appeals to gas, electricity, telephone, food, and fuel functionaries; the other in trying to buy things that could not be bought. In the evenings they scrubbed the floors, painted the walls, and ate bread and margarine. All their friends told them how lucky they were, and asked if they had any rooms to spare.

The faintly distressing smell they had rented with the house did not diminish. Charles said Mrs. Smith had run away, not to find romance, but to escape the smell.

Charles found it was impossible to turn on the bath faucets without taking off his shoes and standing in the bath. When he had done this he found that the pipes had been disconnected. He agreed that the bath must be moved.

It took them four hours to haul the bathtub upstairs: some of that time was spent in offering each other conflicting advice at the corners, but there was enough hard work to make Charles feel that his heart was affected. He sat trembling on the edge of the bathtub, while Greta went to make some tea.

She came upstairs without the tea and stood silent for so long that her husband began to feel nervous.

"I think you should have a look at the bathroom, not this bathroom, the other one," she said in a thin voice. His smothered thoughts leaped to the surface as he stared at her. She nodded.

"The tiles underneath the bath," she said. "I noticed they were loose, now that we'd moved it. I picked one out—you'd better come see."

He went downstairs. Greta led him to the spot where the bathtub had been. Yes, the tiles underneath it had been taken up and relaid. Clumsily.

"That's why the pipes were disconnected," Greta said behind him. "The bath had already been moved once before and put back. Lift up that loose tile and look."

He did so. His face was a bit green as he backed out and he and Greta went upstairs again. Neither of them spoke for some minutes. They were thinking of real estate agents, furniture stores, gas and electricity men, food and fuel offices, carpenters, builders, pots of paint, stacks of bread and margarine. They were thinking of the quiet and orderly lives they had once led, and of how they had never done anyone any harm. They were thinking of how impossible it would be to find another house in London as it was today.

Charles sat stiff and still. He hoped he would never be asked to get up, to speak, to act. Unpleasant as this moment was, he wanted it to last as long as his life and not be succeeded by any kind of future.

"Do you think the shops are shut?" Greta asked. "We could get some cement from the builder's," she said. "Or something airtight. I think jobs like that should be done properly." She smoothed her hair and hummed a little. "I'll make some tea while you go for the cement."

That night, when the rest of the work was over, they moved the bath downstairs again. The neighbors were curious about the noise, but they never learned what had caused it. This was just as well, for if any rumors had reached the ears of Mr. Smith, he would have been most upset.

Mrs. Smith was past caring.

The Uninvited

MICHAEL GILBERT

Mr. Calder was silent, solitary and generous with everything, from a basket of cherries or mushrooms, to efficient first aid to a child who had tumbled. The children liked him. But their admiration was reserved for his dog.

The great, solemn, sagacious Rasselas was a deerhound. He had been born in the sunlight. His coat was the color of dry sherry, his nose was blue-black and his eyes shone like worked amber. From the neat tufts at his heels to the top of his dome-shaped head, there was a royalty about him. He had lived in courts and consorted on his own terms with other princes.

Mr. Calder's cottage stood at the top of a fold in the Kentish Downs. The road curled up to it from Lamperdown, in the valley. First it climbed slowly between woods, then forked sharply left and rose steeply, coming out onto the plateau, rounded and clear as a bald pate. The road served only the cottage, and stopped in front of its gate.

Beyond the house, there were paths which led through the home fields and into the woods beyond, woods full of primroses, bluebells, pheasant's eggs, chestnuts, hollow trees and ghosts. The woods did not belong to Mr. Calder. They belonged, in theory, to a syndicate of businessmen from the Medway towns, who came at the week ends, in autumn and winter, to kill birds. When the sound of their shooting brakes announced their arrival, Mr. Calder would call Rasselas indoors. At all other times, the great dog roamed freely in the garden and in the three open fields which formed Mr. Calder's domain. But he never went out of sight of the house, nor beyond the sound of his master's voice.

The children said that the dog talked to the man, and this was perhaps not far from the truth. Before Mr. Calder came, the cottage had been inhabited by a bad-tempered oaf who had looked on himself as custodian for the Medway sportsmen, and had chased and harried the children who, in their turn, had become adept at avoiding him.

When Mr. Calder first came, they had spent a little time in trying him, before finding him harmless. Nor had it taken them long to find out something else. No one could cross the plateau unobserved, small though he might be and quietly though he might move. A pair of sensitive ears would have heard, a pair of amber eyes would have seen; and Rasselas would pad in at the open door and look enquiringly at Mr. Calder who would say, "Yes, it's the Lightfoot boys and their sister. I saw them, too." And Rasselas would stalk out and lie down again in his favorite day bed, on the sheltered side of the woodpile.

Apart from the children, visitors to the cottage were a rarity. The postman wheeled his bicycle up the hill once a day; delivery vans appeared at their appointed times; the fish man on Tuesdays, the grocer on Thursdays, the butcher on Fridays. In the summer, occasional hikers wandered past, unaware that their approach, their passing, and their withdrawal had all been reported to the owner of the cottage.

Mr. Calder's only regular visitor was Mr. Behrens, the retired schoolmaster, who lived in the neck of the valley, two hundred yards outside Lamperdown Village, in a house which had once been the Rectory. Mr. Behrens kept bees, and lived with his aunt. His forward-stooping head, his wrinkled, brown skin, blinking eyes and cross expression made him look like a tortoise which has been roused untimely from its winter sleep.

Once or twice a week, summer and winter, Mr. Behrens would get out his curious tweed hat and his iron-tipped walking stick, and would go tip-tapping up the hill to have tea with Mr. Calder. The dog knew and tolerated Mr. Behrens, who would scratch his ears and say, "Rasselas. Silly name. *You* came from Persia, not Abyssinia." It was believed that the two old gentlemen played backgammon.

There were other peculiarities about Mr. Calder's ménage which were not quite so very apparent to the casual onlooker.

When he first took over the house, some of the alterations he had asked for had caused Mr. Benskin, the builder, to scratch his head. Why, for instance, had he wanted one perfectly good southern-facing window filled in, and two more opened, on the north side of the house?

Mr. Calder had been vague. He said that he liked an all-round view and plenty of fresh air. In which case, asked Mr. Benskin, why had he insisted on heavy shutters on all downstairs windows and a steel plate behind the woodwork of the front and back doors?

There had also been the curious matter of the telephone line. When Mr. Calder had mentioned that he was having the telephone installed, Mr. Benskin had laughed. The post office, overwhelmed as they were with post-war work, were hardly likely to carry their line of poles a full mile up the hill for one solitary cottage. But Mr. Benskin had been wrong, and on two counts. Not only had the post office installed a telephone, with surprising promptness, but they had actually dug a trench and brought it in underground.

When this was reported to him, Mr. Benskin had told the public ear of the Golden Lion that he had always known there was something odd about Mr. Calder.

"He's an inventor," he said. "To my mind, there's no doubt that's what he is. An inventor. He's got government support. Otherwise, how'd he get a telephone line laid like that?"

Had Mr. Benskin been able to observe Mr. Calder getting out of bed in the morning, he would have been fortified in his opinion. For it is a well-known fact that inventors are odd, and Mr. Calder's routine on rising was very odd indeed.

Summer and winter, he would wake half an hour before dawn. He turned on no electric light. Instead, armed with a big torch, he would pad downstairs, the cold nose of Rasselas a few inches behind him, and make a minute inspection of the three ground-floor rooms. On the edges of the shutters were certain tiny, thread-like wires, almost invisible to the naked eye. When he had satisfied himself that these were in order, Mr. Calder would return upstairs and get dressed.

By this time, day was coming up. The darkness had withdrawn across the bare meadow and chased the ghosts back into the surrounding woods. Mr. Calder would take a pair of heavy naval binoculars from his dressing table, and, sitting back from the window, would study with care the edges of his domain. Nothing escaped his attention: a wattle hurdle blocking a path; a bent sapling at the edge of the glade; a scut of fresh earth in the hedge. The inspection was repeated from the window on the opposite side.

Then, whistling softly to himself, Mr. Calder would walk downstairs to cook breakfast for himself and for Rasselas.

The postman, who arrived at eleven o'clock, brought the newspapers with the letters. Perhaps because he lived alone and saw so few people, Mr. Calder seemed particularly fond of his letters and papers. He opened them with a loving care which an observer might have found ludicrous. His fingers caressed the envelope, or the wrapping paper, very gently, as a man will squeeze a cigar. Often he would hold an envelope up to the light as if he could read, through the outer covering, the message inside. Sometimes, he would even weigh an envelope in the delicate letter scales which he kept on top of his desk between a stuffed seagull and a night-scented jasmine in a pot.

On a fine morning in May, when the sun was fulfilling, in majesty, the promise of a misty dawn, Mr. Calder unfolded his copy of the *Times*, turned, as was his custom, to the foreign news pages, and started to read.

He had stretched his hand out toward his coffee cup when he stopped. It was a tiny check, a break in the natural sequence of his actions, but it was enough to make Rasselas look up. Mr. Calder smiled reassuringly at the dog. His hand resumed its movement, picked up the cup, carried it to his mouth. But the dog was not easy.

Mr. Calder read, once more, the five-line item which had caught his attention. Then he glanced at his watch, went across to the telephone, dialed a Lamperdown number and spoke to Jack, at the garage, which also ran a taxi service.

"Just do it if we hurry," said Jack. "No time to spare. I'll come right up."

While he waited for the taxi, Mr. Calder first telephoned Mr. Behrens, to warn him that they might have to postpone their game of backgammon. Then he spent a little time telling Rasselas that he was leaving him in charge of the cottage, but that he would be back before dark. Rasselas swept the carpet with his feathery tail, and made no attempt to follow Mr. Calder when Jack's Austin came charging up the hill and reversed in front of the cottage gate.

In the end, the train was ten minutes late at the junction, and Mr. Calder caught it with ease.

He got out at Victoria, walked down Victoria Street, turned to the right, opposite the open space where the Colonial Office used to stand, and to the right again into the Square. In the southwest corner stands the Westminister branch of the London and Home Counties Bank.

Mr. Calder walked into the bank. The head cashier, Mr. Macleod, nodded gravely to him and said, "Mr. Fortescue is ready. You can go straight in."

"I'm afraid the train was late," said Mr. Calder. "We lost ten minutes at the junction, and never caught it up."

"Trains are not as reliable now as they used to be," agreed Mr. Macleod.

A young lady from a nearby office had just finished banking the previous day's takings. Mr. Macleod was watching her out of the corner of his eye until the door had shut behind her. Then he said, with exactly the same inflection, but more softly, "Will it be necessary to make any special arrangements for your departure?"

"Oh, no, thank you," said Mr. Calder. "I took all the necessary precautions."

"Fine," said Mr. Macleod.

He held open the heavy door, paneled in sham walnut in the style affected by pre-war bank designers, ushered Mr. Calder into the anteroom and left him there for a few moments, in contemplation of its only ornament, a reproduction, in a massive gilt frame, of Landseer's allegory "The Tug of War." Thrift and Industry appeared to be gaining a hard-fought victory over Luxury and Extravagance.

Then the head cashier reappeared and held open the door for Mr. Calder.

Mr. Fortescue, who came forward to greet him, would have been identified in any company as a bank manager. It was not only the conventional dress, the square, sagacious face, the suggestion that as soon as his office door closed behind him, he would extract an old pipe and push it into his discreet but friendly mouth. It was more than that. It was the bearing, the balance, the air of certainty and stability in a dubious and unstable world, which sits upon a man when he is the representative of a corporation with a hundred million pounds of disclosed assets.

"Nice to see you," he said. "Grab a chair. Any trouble on the way up?"

"No trouble," said Mr. Calder. "I don't think anything can start for another two or three weeks."

"They might have post-dated the item to put you off your guard." He picked up his own copy of the *Times* and re-read the four and a half lines of print which recorded that Colonel Josef Weinleben, the international expert on bacterial antibodies, had died in Klagenfurt as the result of an abdominal operation.

"No," said Calder. "He wanted me to read it, and sweat."

"It would be the established procedure to organize his own 'death' before setting on a serious mission," Mr. Fortescue agreed. He picked up a heavy paper knife and tapped thoughtfully with it on the desk. "But it could be true, this time. Weinleben must be nearly sixty."

"He's coming," said Mr. Calder. "I can feel it in my bones. It may even be true that he's ill. If he was dying, he'd like to take me along with him."

"What makes you so sure?"

"I tortured him," said Mr. Calder. "And broke him. He'd never forget."

"No," said Mr. Fortescue. He held the point of the paper knife toward the window, sighting down it as if it had been a pistol. "No. I think very likely you're right. We'll try to pick him up at the port, and tag him. But we can't guarantee to stop him getting in. If he tries to operate, of course, he'll have to show his hand. You've got your permanent cover. Do you want anything extra?"

He might, thought Mr. Calder, have been speaking to a customer. You've got your normal overdraft. Do you want any extra accommodation, Mr. Calder? The bank is here to serve you. There was something at the same time ridiculous and comforting in treating life and death as though they were entries in the same balance sheet.

"I'm not at all sure that I want you to stop him," he

said. "We aren't at war. You could only deport him. It might be more satisfactory to let him through."

"Do you know," said Mr. Fortescue, "the same thought had occurred to me."

Mrs. Farmer, who kept the Seven Gables Guest House, between Aylesford and Bearsted, considered Mr. Wendon a perfect guest. His passport and the card which he had duly filled in on arrival showed him to be a Dutchman; but his English, though accented in odd places, was colloquial and fluent. An upright, red-faced, gray-haired man, he was particularly nice with Mrs. Farmer's two young children. Moreover, he gave no trouble. He was—and this was a sovereign virtue in Mrs. Farmer's eyes—methodical and predictable.

Every morning, in the endless succession of the fine days which heralded that summer, he would go out walking, clad in aged but respectable tweed, field glasses over one shoulder, a small knapsack on the other for camera, sandwiches, and thermos flask. And in the evenings, he would sit in the lounge, drinking a single glass of schnapps as an aperitif before dinner, and entertaining Tom and Rebecca with accounts of the birds he had observed that day. It was difficult to imagine, seeing him sitting there, gentle, placid, and upright, that he had killed men and women—and children, too—with his own well-kept hands. But then Mr. Wendon, or Weinleben, or Weber, was a remarkable man.

On the tenth day of his stay, he received a letter from Holland. Its contents seemed to cause him some satisfaction, and he read it twice before putting it away in his wallet. The stamps he tore off, giving them to Mrs. Farmer for Tom.

"I may be a little late this evening," he said. "I am meeting a friend at Maidstone. Don't keep dinner for me."

That morning, he packed his knapsack with particular care and caught the Maidstone bus at Aylesford crossroads. He had said that he was going to Maidstone and he never told unnecessary lies.

After that, his movements became somewhat complicated, but by four o'clock, he was safely ensconced in a dry ditch to the north of the old Rectory at Lamperdown. Here he consumed a biscuit, and observed the front drive of the house.

At a quarter past four, Jack arrived with his taxi and Mr. Behren's aunt came out, wearing, despite the heat of the day, coat and gloves and a rather saucy scarf, and was installed in the back seat. Mr. Behrens handed in her shopping basket, waved goodbye, and retired into the house.

Five minutes later, Mr. Wendon was knocking at the front door. Mr. Behrens opened it, and blinked when he saw the gun in his visitor's hand.

"I must ask you to turn around and walk in front of me," said Mr. Wendon.

"Why should I?" said Mr. Behrens. He sounded more irritated than alarmed.

"If you don't, I shall shoot you," said Mr. Wendon. He said it exactly as if he meant it and pushed Mr. Behrens toward a door.

After a moment, Mr. Behrens wheeled about, and asked, "Where now?"

"That looks the sort of place I had in mind," said Mr. Wendon. "Open the door and walk in. But quite slowly."

It was a small, dark room, devoted to hats, coats, sticks, old tennis rackets, croquet mallets, bee veils, and such.

"Excellent," said Mr. Wendon. He helped himself to the old-fashioned tweed hat and the iron-tipped walking stick which Mr. Behrens carried abroad with him on all his perambulations of the countryside. "A small window, and a stout, old door. What could be better?"

Still watching Mr. Behrens closely, he laid the hat and stick on the hall table, dipped his left hand into his own coat pocket and brought out a curious-looking metal object.

"You have not, perhaps, seen one of these before? It works on the same principle as a Mills grenade, but is six times as powerful and is incendiary as well as explosive. When I shut this door, I shall bolt it and hang the grenade from the upturned bolt. The least disturbance will dislodge it. It is powerful enough to blow the door down."

"All right," said Mr. Behrens. "But get on with it. My sister will be back soon."

"Not until eight o'clock, if she adheres to last week's arrangements," said Mr. Wendon quite knowingly

He closed the door, shot the bolts, top and bottom, and

suspended the grenade with artistic care from the top one.

Mr. Calder had finished his tea by five o'clock, and then shortly afterward strolled down to the end of the paddock, where he was repairing the fence. Rasselas lay quietly in the lee of the wood pile. The golden afternoon turned imperceptibly toward evening.

Rasselas wrinkled his velvet muzzle to dislodge a fly. On one side, he could hear Mr. Calder digging with his mattock into the hilltop chalk and grunting as he dug. Behind, some four fields away, a horse, fly-plagued, was kicking its heels and bucking. Then, away to his left, he located a familiar sound. The clink of an iron-tipped walking stick on stone.

Rasselas liked to greet the arrival of this particular friend of his master, but he waited, with dignity, until the familiar tweed had come into view. Then he unfolded himself and trotted gently out into the road.

So strong was the force of custom, so disarming were the familiar and expected sight and sound, that even Rasselas' five senses were lulled. But his instinct was awake. The figure was still a dozen paces off and advancing confidently, when Rasselas stopped. His eyes searched the figure. Right appearance, right hat, right noises. But wrong gait. Quicker, and more purposeful than their old friend. And, above all, wrong smell.

The dog hackled, then crouched as if to jump. But it was the man who jumped. He leaped straight at the dog, his hand came out from under his coat and the loaded stick hissed through the air with brutal force. Rasselas was still moving, and the blow missed his head, but struck him full on the back of the neck. He went down without a sound.

Mr. Calder finished digging the socket for the corner post he was planting, straightened his back and decided that he would fetch the brush and creosote from the house. As he came out of the paddock, he saw the great dog lying in the road.

He ran forward and knelt in the dust. There was no need to look twice.

He hardly troubled to raise his eyes when a voice which he recognized spoke from behind him.

"Keep your hands in sight," said Colonel Weinleben,

"and try not to make any sudden or unexpected move."

Mr. Calder got up.

"I suggest we move back into the house," said the colonel. "We shall be more private there. I should like to devote at least as much attention to you as you did to me on the last occasion we met."

Mr. Calder seemed hardly to be listening. He was looking down at the crumpled, empty, tawny skin, incredibly changed by the triviality of life's departure. His eyes were full of tears.

"You killed him," he said.

"As I shall shortly kill you," said the colonel. And as he spoke, he spun round like a startled marionette, took a stiff pace forward and fell, face downward.

Mr. Calder looked at him incuriously. From the shattered hole in the side of his head, dark blood ran out and mixed with the white dust. Rasselas had not bled at all. He was glad of that tiny distinction between the two deaths.

It was Mr. Behrens who had killed Colonel Weinleben, with a single shot from a .312 rifle, fired from the edge of the wood. The rifle was fitted with a telescopic sight, but the shot was a fine one, even for an excellent marksman such as Mr. Behrens.

He'd run for nearly a quarter of a mile before firing it; he had to get into position very quickly, and he had only just been able to see the colonel's head over the top of an intervening hedge.

He burst through this hedge now, saw Rasselas, and started to curse.

"It wasn't your fault," said Mr. Calder. He was sitting in the road, the dog's head in his lap.

"If I'm meant to look after you, I ought to look after you properly," said Mr. Behrens. "Not let myself be jumped by an amateur like that. I hadn't reckoned on him blocking the door with a grenade. I had to break out of the window, and it took me nearly half an hour."

"We've a lot to do," said Mr. Calder He got stiffly to his feet and went to fetch a spade.

Between them they dug a deep grave, behind the wood pile, and laid the dog in it, and filled it in, and patted the earth into a mound. It was a fine resting place, looking out southward over the feathery tops of the trees, across the Weald of Kent. A resting place for a prince.

Colonel Weinleben they buried later, with a good deal more haste and less ceremony, in the wood. He was the illegitimate son of a cobbler from Mainz and greatly inferior to the dog, both in birth and breeding.

The Substance of Martyrs

WILLIAM SAMBROT

For centuries, the townspeople had held on to their belief in the powers of their gold cross. What a sublime ironic touch that the ravages of a war "to end all wars" brought an answer to their prayers.

For reasons that will be apparent to you, I won't tell you the name of the little German village in which I saw the miraculous golden Christ on the cross. It's an obscure, somewhat poor hamlet, still not completely recovered from the ravages of World War II.

It was Colonel Dumphrey who told me about the golden Christ, and the strange history of miracles attributed to it. We were motoring through southern Germany at the time, on our way from Paris to Salzburg, where the colonel was to pass judgment on the authenticity of certain art treasures recently discovered in a salt mine near Salzburg.

Colonel Dumphrey (retired), D.S.O., O.B.E., was (and is) a renowned scholar and linguist, an expert on Italian Renaissance and Middle-European medieval art. During the war, Colonel Dumphrey had been a major in Military Intelligence (British Army), on special detached duty with the 45th Division (American).

Near the end of World War II, the 45th had captured a number of salt mines near Salzburg crammed with a vast quantity of loot which the Nazis had stolen from Europe's finest museums and private art collections.

To this day, not all the treasures known to have been stolen by the Nazis have been recovered, so when the colonel was contacted in Paris and asked to give his expert opinion on the authenticity of the several pieces which had recently been found in those same dismal salt mines, he readily agreed.

He decided to drive up from Paris to Salzburg, taking his time and visiting some of the lesser-known but still interesting German and Austrian towns, so rich in medieval art. He invited me along.

We were well into southern Germany, meandering through Christmas card villages, driving through a peaceful, sparsely-inhabited mountainous country, when suddenly the colonel slowed as we approached a road sign.

He hesitated, then abruptly swung the car off onto a bumpy road. Ahead, there soon appeared the inevitable clump of stone-and-timber houses. In their midst, the spire of a small cathedral thrust up, peculiarly truncated.

As we approached, it was evident the church had been heavily damaged during the war and still lacked complete repair. Several of the stained-glass Gothic apertures had been boarded up. The slate roof showed evidence of frequent mismatched patching. All in all, a rather humble and shabby church and village, tucked between the mountains. And yet . . .

Miraculous cures had taken place there, Dumphrey assured me. People came from many hundreds of miles around to pray before the little church's altar crucifix, a solid gold Christ on the cross. To pray for—and occasionally to receive—miracles.

We got out of the car and immediately I was struck by the feeling of peace and tranquility that flooded the square, the town. People smiled at us, moved quietly in unhurried calm. Most of them were going to or from the church.

We went in. It was very much like many other churches throughout western Europe—a bit more brown and battered, perhaps. Many pews were scarred, a few were new. The floor showed patches of repaired tile, contrasting with ancient marble. To one side, a stained-glass window was oddly shattered; only two pieces remained suspended between the lead frames, each depicting an upraised, supplicating hand. The rest was opened to the sky.

Pigeons fluttered in and out between these suspended marvelously-colored stained-glass hands. Hands, Dumphrey whispered, which formerly belonged to a complete Mary, mother of Christ, but now were disembodied members, raised piteously to an uncomprehending stretch of blue, cold German sky.

The shattered stained-glass window was the people's monument to their bitter past—their penance, and their reminder. It was left exactly as it had been when the war swept over it.

Here the parishioners and visitors knelt on the marble floor, oblivious of the chill wind that swept through the broken window and caused the red sacristy lamp to flicker and sway ceaselessly.

Directly above the chipped altar was hung the magnificent crucifix. A great golden Christ, nailed to a mahogany cross. The outstretched arms seemed to steady and make firm the sagging church walls. It glowed in the flickering light of candles; the flaring shadows made the suffering features strangely alive. The closed eyes seemed to slowly open, to look down on the kneeling people, and gradually, to seek me out.

I had seen many excellent crucifixes. But I found myself staring piercingly at the golden Christ, hanging tautly, corded arms nailed with golden spikes to the dark wood. There flowed from that strained figure an unmistakable aura. It was palpable: I felt that the closed eyes were no longer closed, but were gazing at me—into me—with pity and love.

My heart began a slow, deep pound; I could have sworn I saw the golden ribs heave, the cruel deep spear marks gape wide. I continued to stare at the cross, barely conscious of the muted surf-sound of murmured prayers, the fluttering and cooing of pigeons. All was subordinate to that lonely, mysterious figure, hanging there, beckoning with a power that was indescribably real.

Dumphrey touched my arm and I started. We went outside and I took a deep breath.

"It—it's magnificent," I said slowly. "There *is* something —some presence there. Did you feel it?"

He nodded and I said, "I can rationalize it, I suppose. Mass hypnosis, that gleaming body concentrating the flickering light . . . But that . . . that feeling of utter peace, a profound sense of . . . of . . ."

"Love?" Dumphrey said.

"Yes. A deep, calm love. An acceptance." I glanced back. "I can readily understand why these people will come from miles away to kneel beneath that crucifix." I stopped. Dumphrey was lighting his pipe thoughtfully. "It must be beyond value to them. I have the feeling that it's very old."

"No," he said. "This one dates back to nineteen forty-five."

"*This* one?"

"There was another, exactly like this one," Dumphrey said. "And it was really old, dating back, I'm sure, to medieval times."

"What happened to it?" I said. "Was it solid gold, like this one?"

He looked at me, a rather odd look. "The villagers always thought so," he said.

They were proud of their crucifix, Dumphrey told me, standing there on the steps. Gleaming brilliantly in the candlelight, the great golden crucifix had always hung in their church—far beyond the memory of the oldest living inhabitant. It was the most precious object in their lives; not only because they believed it to be pure gold, but because it symbolized the complete unity of their faith. Even though the church doors were never locked and strangers never refused admittance, their crucifix had never been disturbed. Never.

But then no wars had ever really touched this hamlet. No wars, that is, until Hitler proclaimed his right to rule the world. Then war came to the village with a vengeance—and only after it was already lost for Germany and very bad for everyone.

With all the strong young men long since gone—killed or captured on the many fronts—there were only the *Herrenvolk* left to fight. The People's Army. The halt, the misfit, the old—the dregs of humanity. Poor fighting material, perhaps, but over them were placed the most brutal and fanatical of Hitler's officers: the dreaded Waffen S.S., Hitler's elite killer corps. Men sworn to defend the fatherland to the death.

Untersturmfuhrer Hohler, former assistant commandant at the infamous Dachau concentration camp (then already overrun) was given the job of fortifying the village and assuring that the *Herrenvolk* would, if necessary, fight to the death in its defense.

Hohler fortified the town. Ignoring the protests of the priest and parishioners, he gave orders to use the belltower of the church as a spotting post for their deadly .88 artillery. When the first American light armor approached the town, they were quickly knocked out by a hail of accurate artillery fire. They withdrew, calling on their own artillery for support. There was no choice but to reduce the belltower to rubble.

On a cold February morning, the American units of the 45th whirled through the thin snow in a swift flanking movement and the town was taken. Most of the *Herrenvolk* surrendered immediately. *Untersturmfuhrer* Hohler was not among them. He'd escaped.

The main body of troops moved on, but a few rendezvoused before the church. A young infantry captain, his hands blue with cold, brought an old priest to see then-Major Dumphrey. Anguished, obviously in deep distress, the priest requested in a halting whisper that Dumphrey go with him into the ruined church.

Dumphrey went into the shattered building, past the broken pews and the smashed windows, over bits of blasted stained glass, littering the floor like sharded rainbows.

The priest pointed to the wall above the chipped altar. "We have had a cross there for many centuries," he said in a choked voice. "It was gold, pure gold. No one had ever touched it, though the doors were never locked. And when the shelling came, even though everything else fell, it was untouched. A miracle," he whispered. "It made us humble, and sure that God was protecting us. But now—" His finger trembled.

The wall above the altar was intact, but strangely bare-looking. Against the dark smudge of centuries of candle smoke was the pale outline of where the great gold crucifix had hung. The crucifix was gone.

"*Untersturmfuhrer* Hohler has taken it," the priest cried brokenly.

Hohler: *Untersturmfuhrer,* wearing the lapels of the dreaded *Schutzstaffeln;* assistant commandant at Dachau, specialist in death. The executioner of hundreds of thousands of Jews, a man with a dossier of crimes equaling in length the appalling list of names of his murdered victims. Even then, wanted by the Allies for trial (and subsequent hanging), even at the moment of his personal *Gotterdammerung,* Hohler could not resist adding the gold Christ to his already immense pile of loot.

"We'll get him," the young captain assured his priest. "Where can he run now?"

They got him, near Salzburg. Hohler readily admitted taking the crucifix, and when the indignant young captain brusquely ordered him to hand it over, Hohler laughed ironically, saying he no longer had it—that he'd thrown it away. However, a number of pure gold bars were found in his loot, at least equaling in weight the approximate mass that the melted-down Christ would have been. When questioned at length about this gold, Hohler, after some hesitation, admitted that the gold bars were, indeed, the melted-down remains of the stolen golden Christ.

Fortunately, the exact dimensions of the original Christ had been known and there were any number of skilled carvers in the village capable of making a mold. When the finished Christ was again ready to be hung for the Bishop's blessing, the worshipers more than filled the church. Children in the pews sniffled in the great cold that filled the shattered church. Shuffling and whispering, they stared in awe at the beautiful gleaming crucifix which hung once again above the chipped altar.

The adults knelt silently on the broken floor, enveloped in layers of clothing. Bitter drafts whistled through the empty windows. But it was a church again—their church.

Above the altar that strangely serene, that powerful golden figure enveloped them in a warmth they'd never known before.

And as if to prove that God was indeed among them, there occurred then the first of the miracles attributed to the golden Christ. A child, a victim of the shelling attack, had been brought to the service. The child had been buried alive in the ruins of his blasted home, pinned beneath the bodies of his parents. When they'd dug him out, he had shrieked once, then it was as though a light had been extinguished within him: his eyes went blank. He became mute, an unresisting, unsmiling creature, with no spark of humanity.

But in the church he'd looked upon the golden Christ. A faint light leaped into his eyes. He stared. His eyes became brighter. Brighter. And suddenly he screamed, a terrible, piercing scream. He began to cry. The tears were real, genuine tears of emotion. He was alive again, a thinking, feeling human soul; in great anguish—but sane.

"He is a strong young man now, with children of his own," Dumphrey finished, as we walked down the worn stone steps and back to the car. "His was the first, but there have been similar. . . cures."

"I don't doubt it," I said. "Not any more."

We got into the car and Dumphrey looked reflectively at the people coming and going.

"But he lied, you know," Dumphrey said softly. "*Untersturmfuhrer* Hohler, I mean."

"Lied? In what way?"

Dumphrey brought out his pipe, and stuffing it with tobacco he said slowly, "I don't need to tell you to be discreet about this, of course." He sighed. "Actually, even before Hohler was captured I'd already come into possession of the real stolen crucifix. It had been found by one of my team of specialists."

He made a wry face. "It had been mutilated so badly there was no thought of ever returning it to the church. The arms were twisted and bent, the torso battered, and the crown of thorns torn completely off the head."

"Hohler had actually thrown away the golden Christ?"

"Yes. After he discovered it wasn't gold at all," Dumphrey said. "Where the crown of thorns had been torn off showed dull gray. Where the arms had been twisted and bent, ugly black cracks showed through." He shook his head. "It was merely heavily-gilded lead."

"But—Hohler's gold bars—"

"Can't you guess where that gold came from?" Dumphrey said. "Hohler was one of the butchers of Dachau. Stripping the rings from his victims' fingers as they were led wailing into the gas chambers. Wrenching the gold teeth and fillings from their lifeless mouths as they were fed into the furnaces. Accumulating his pile of gold, melting it down into bars—"

"From the Jews . . ." I whispered.

"Yes, from the martyred Jews of Dachau," Dumphrey said. "Doubtless Hohler considered it a diabolical joke, saying the gold came from the stolen Christ. *But was he so far wrong?*"

He put the little car in gear and we moved slowly out of

the village. "The pagan executioner stole from the Christians their Christ of gilded lead—only to replace it with one made of that most precious metal of all: the substance of martyrs."

Don't Look Behind You

FREDERIC BROWN

Just sit back and relax, now. Try to enjoy this; it's going be the last story you ever read, or nearly the last. After you finish it you can sit there and stall a while, you can find excuses to hang around your house, or your room, or your office, wherever you're reading this; but sooner or later you're going to have to get up and go out. That's where I'm waiting for you: outside. Or maybe closer than that. Maybe in this room.

You think that's a joke of course. You think this is just a story in a book, and that I don't really mean you. Keep right on thinking so. But be fair; admit that I'm giving you fair warning.

Harley bet me I couldn't do it. He bet me a diamond he's told me about, a diamond as big as his head. So you see why I've got to kill you. And why I've got to tell you how and why and all about it first. That's part of the bet. It's just the kind of idea Harley would have.

I'll tell you about Harley first. He's tall and handsome, and suave and cosmopolitan. He looks something like Ronald Coleman, only he's taller. He dresses like a million dollars, but it wouldn't matter if he didn't; I mean that he'd look distinguished in overalls. There's a sort of magic about Harley, a mocking magic in the way he looks at you; it makes you think of palaces and far-off countries and bright music.

It was in Springfield, Ohio, that he met Justin Dean. Justin was a funny-looking little runt who was just a printer. He worked for the Atlas Printing & Engraving Company. He was a very ordinary little guy, just about as different as possible from Harley; you couldn't pick two men more different. He was only thirty-five, but he was mostly bald already, and he had to wear thick glasses because he'd worn out his eyes doing fine printing and engraving. He was a good printer and engraver; I'll say that for him.

I never asked Harley how he happened to come to Springfield, but the day he got there, after he'd checked in at the Castle Hotel, he stopped in at Atlas to have some calling cards made. It happened that Justin Dean was alone in the shop at the time, and he took Harley's order for the cards; Harley wanted engraved ones, the best. Harley always wants the best of everything.

Harley probably didn't even notice Justin; there was no reason why he should have. But Justin noticed Harley all right, and in him he saw everything that he himself would like to be, and never would be, because most of the things Harley has, you have to be born with.

And Justin made the plates for the cards himself and printed them himself, and he did a wonderful job—something he thought would be worthy of a man like Harley Prentice. That was the name engraved on the card, just that and nothing else, as all really important people have their cards engraved.

He did fine-line work on it, freehand cursive style, and used all the skill he had. It wasn't wasted, because the next day when Harley called to get the cards he held one and stared at it for a while, and then he looked at Justin, seeing him for the first time. He asked, "Who did this?"

And little Justin told him proudly who had done it, and Harley smiled at him and told him it was the work of an artist, and he asked Justin to have dinner with him that evening after work, in the Blue Room of the Castle Hotel.

That's how Harley and Justin got together, but Harley was careful. He waited until he'd known Justin a while before he asked him whether or not he could make plates for five and ten dollar bills. Harley had the contacts; he could market the bills in quantity with men who specialized in passing them, and—most important—he knew where he could get paper with the silk threads in it, paper that wasn't quite the genuine thing, but was close enough to pass inspection by anyone but an expert.

So Justin quit his job at Atlas and he and Harley went to New York, and they set up a little printing shop as a blind, on Amsterdam Avenue south of Sherman Square, and they worked at the bills. Justin worked hard, harder than he had ever worked in his life, because besides working on the plates for the bills, he helped meet expenses by handling what legitimate printing work came into the shop.

He worked day and night for almost a year, making plate after plate, and each one was a little better than the last, and finally he had plates that Harley said were good enough. That night they had dinner at the Waldorf-Astoria to celebrate and after dinner they went the rounds of the best night clubs, and it cost Harley a small fortune, but that didn't matter because they were going to get rich.

They drank champagne, and it was the first time Justin ever drank champagne and he got disgustingly drunk and must have made quite a fool of himself. Harley told him about it afterwards, but Harley wasn't mad at him. He took him back to his room at the hotel and put him to bed, and Justin was pretty sick for a couple of days. But that didn't matter, either, because they were going to get rich.

Then Justin started printing bills from the plates, and they got rich. After that, Justin didn't have to work so hard, either, because he turned down most jobs that came into the print shop, told them he was behind schedule and couldn't handle any more. He took just a little work, to keep up a front. And behind the front, he made five and ten dollar bills, and he and Harley got rich.

He got to know other people whom Harley knew. He met Bull Mallon, who handled the distribution end. Bull Mallon was built like a bull, that was why they called him that. He had a face that never smiled or changed expression at all except when he was holding burning matches to the soles of Justin's bare feet. But that wasn't then; that was later, when he wanted Justin to tell him where the plates were.

And he got to know Captain John Willys of the Police Department, who was a friend of Harley's, to whom Harley gave quite a bit of the money they made, but that didn't matter either, because there was plenty left and they all got rich. He met a friend of Harley's who was a big star of the stage, and one who owned a big New York newspaper. He got to know other people equally important, but in less respectable ways.

Harley, Justin knew, had a hand in lots of other enter-rises besides the little mint on Amsterdam Avenue. Some f these ventures took him out of town, usually over weeknds. And the weekend that Harley was murdered Justin ever found out what really happened, except that Harley 'ent away and didn't come back. Oh, he knew that he was ıurdered, all right, because the police found his body—vith three bullet holes in his chest—in the most expensive uite of the best hotel in Albany. Even for a place to be ound dead in Harley Prentice had chosen the best.

All Justin ever knew about it was that a long distance all came to him at the hotel where he was staying, the ight that Harley was murdered—it must have been a mater of minutes, in fact, before the time the newspapers said Iarley was killed.

It was Harley's voice on the phone, and his voice was lebonair and unexcited as ever. But he said, "Justin? Get o the shop and get rid of the plates, the paper, everything. Right away. I'll explain when I see you." He waited only ıntil Justin said, "Sure, Harley," and then he said, "Ataboy," and hung up.

Justin hurried around to the printing shop and got the olates and the paper and a few thousand dollars' worth of counterfeit bills that were on hand. He made the paper and oills into one bundle and the copper plates into another, maller one, and he left the shop with no evidence that it ıad ever been a mint in miniature.

He was very careful and very clever in disposing of both oundles. He got rid of the big one first by checking in at a oig hotel, not one he or Harley ever stayed at, under a 'alse name, just to have a chance to put the big bundle in he incinerator there. It was paper and it would burn. And ıe made sure there was a fire in the incinerator before he lropped it down the chute.

The plates were different. They wouldn't burn, he knew, o he took a trip to Staten Island and back on the ferry ınd, somewhere out in the middle of the bay, he dropped he bundle over the side into the water.

Then, having done what Harley had told him to do, and ıaving done it well and thoroughly, he went back to the ıotel—his own hotel, not the one where he had dumped he paper and the bills—and went to sleep.

In the morning he read in the newspapers that Harley

had been killed, and he was stunned. It didn't seem poss ble. He couldn't believe it; it was a joke someone w. playing on him. Harley would come back to him, he kne And he was right; Harley did, but that was later, in t swamp.

But anyway, Justin had to know, so he took the ve next train for Albany. He must have been on the tra when the police went to his hotel, and at the hotel th must have learned he'd asked at the desk about trains f Albany, because they were waiting for him when he got c the train there.

They took him to a station and they kept him there long long time, days and days, asking him questions. The found out, after a while, that he couldn't have killed Ha ley because he'd been in New York City at the time Harle was killed in Albany but they knew also that he and Ha ley had been operating the little mint, and they thoug that might be a lead to who killed Harley, and they we interested in the counterfeiting, too, maybe even more tha in the murder. They asked Justin Dean questions, over an over and over, and he couldn't answer them, so he didn' They kept him awake for days at a time, asking him que tions over and over. Most of all they wanted to kno where the plates were. He wished he could tell them th the plates were safe where nobody could ever get the again, but he couldn't tell them that without admitting th he and Harley had been counterfeiting, so he couldn't te them.

They located the Amsterdam shop, but they didn't fin any evidence there, and they really had no evidence t hold Justin on at all, but he didn't know that, and it neve occurred to him to get a lawyer.

He kept wanting to see Harley, and they wouldn't l him; then, when they learned he really didn't believe Ha ley could be dead, they made him look at a dead man the said was Harley, and he guessed it was, although Harle looked different dead. He didn't look magnificent, dea And Justin believed, then, but still didn't believe. And afte that he just went silent and wouldn't say a word, eve when they kept him awake for days and days with a brigh light in his eyes, and kept slapping him to keep him awak They didn't use clubs or rubber hoses, but they slappe him a million times and wouldn't let him sleep. And after a while he lost track of things and couldn't have answered their questions even if he'd wanted to.

For a while after that, he was in a bed in a white room, and all he remembers about that are nightmares he had, and calling for Harley and an awful confusion as to whether Harley was dead or not, and then things came back to him gradually and he knew he didn't want to stay in the white room; he wanted to get out so he could hunt for Harley. And if Harley was dead, he wanted to kill whoever had killed Harley, because Harley would have done the same for him.

So he began pretending, and acting, very cleverly, the way the doctors and nurses seemed to want him to act, and after a while they gave him his clothes and let him go.

He was becoming cleverer now. He thought, What would Harley tell me to do? And he knew they'd try to follow him because they'd think he might lead them to the plates, which they didn't know were at the bottom of the bay, and he gave them the slip before he left Albany, and he went first to Boston, and from there by boat to New York, instead of going direct.

He went first to the print shop, and went in the back way after watching the alley for a long time to be sure the place wasn't guarded. It was a mess; they must have searched it very thoroughly for the plates.

Harley wasn't there, of course. Justin left and from a phone booth in a drugstore he telephoned their hotel and asked for Harley and was told Harley no longer lived there; and to be clever and not let them guess who he was, he asked for Justin Dean, and they said Justin Dean didn't live there any more either.

Then he moved to a different drugstore and from there he decided to call up some friends of Harley's, and he phoned Bull Mallon first and because Bull was a friend, he told him who he was and asked if he knew where Harley was.

Bull Mallon didn't pay any attention to that; he sounded excited, a little, and he asked, "Did the cops get the plates, Dean?" and Justin said they didn't, that he wouldn't tell them, and he asked again about Harley.

Bull asked, "Are you nuts, or kidding?" And Justin just asked him again, and Bull's voice changed and he said,

"Where are you?" and Justin told him. Bull said, "Harley's here. He's staying under cover, but it's all right if you know, Dean. You wait right there at the drugstore, and we'll come and get you."

They came and got Justin, Bull Mallon and two other men in a car, and they told him Harley was hiding out way deep in New Jersey and that they were going to drive there now. So he went along and sat in the back seat between two men he didn't know, while Bull Mallon drove.

It was late afternoon then, when they picked him up, and Bull drove all evening and most of the night and he drove fast, so he must have gone farther than New Jersey, at least into Virginia or maybe farther, into the Carolinas.

The sky was getting faintly gray with first dawn when they stopped at a rustic cabin that looked like it had been used as a hunting lodge. It was miles from anywhere, there wasn't even a road leading to it, just a trail that was level enough for the car to be able to make it.

They took Justin into the cabin and tied him to a chair, and they told him Harley wasn't there, but Harley had told them that Justin would tell them where the plates were, and he couldn't leave until he did tell.

Justin didn't believe them; he knew then that they'd tricked him about Harley, but it didn't matter, as far as the plates were concerned. It didn't matter if he told them what he'd done with the plates, because they couldn't get them again, and they wouldn't tell the police. So he told them, quite willingly.

But they didn't believe him. They said he'd hidden the plates and was lying. They tortured him to make him tell. They beat him, and they cut him with knives, and they held burning matches and lighted cigars to the soles of his feet, and they pushed needles under his fingernails. Then they'd rest and ask him questions and if he could talk, he'd tell them the truth, and after a while they'd start to torture him again.

It went on for days and weeks—Justin doesn't know how long, but it was a long time. Once they went away for several days and left him tied up with nothing to eat or drink. They came back and started in all over again. And all the time he hoped Harley would come to help him, but Harley didn't come, not then.

After a while what was happening in the cabin ended, or anyway he didn't know any more about it. They must have thought he was dead; maybe they were right, or anyway not far from wrong.

The next thing he knows was the swamp. He was lying in shallow water at the edge of deeper water. His face was out of the water; it woke him when he turned a little and his face went under. They must have thought him dead and thrown him into the water, but he had floated into the shallow part before he had drowned, and a last flicker of consciousness had turned him over on his back with his face out.

I don't remember much about Justin in the swamp; it was a long time, but I just remember flashes of it. I couldn't move at first; I just lay there in the shallow water with my face out. It got dark and it got cold, I remember, and finally my arms would move a little and I got farther out of the water, lying in the mud with only my feet in the water. I slept or was unconscious again and when I woke up it was getting gray dawn, and that was when Harley came. I think I'd been calling him, and he must have heard.

He stood there, dressed as immaculately and perfectly as ever, right in the swamp, and he was laughing at me for being so weak and lying there like a log, half in the dirty water and half in the mud, and I got up and nothing hurt any more.

We shook hands and he said, "Come on, Justin, let's get you out of here," and I was so glad he'd come that I cried a little. He laughed at me for that and said I should lean on him and he'd help me walk, but I wouldn't do that, because I was coated with mud and filth of the swamp and he was so clean and perfect in a white linen suit, like an ad in a magazine. And all the way out of that swamp, all the days and nights we spent there, he never even got mud on his trouser cuffs, nor his hair mussed.

I told him just to lead the way, and he did, walking just ahead of me, sometimes turning around, laughing and talking to me and cheering me up. Sometimes I'd fall but I wouldn't let him come back and help me. But he'd wait patiently until I could get up. Sometimes I'd crawl instead when I couldn't stand up any more. Sometimes I'd have to swim streams that he'd leap lightly across.

And it was day and night and day and night, and sometimes I'd sleep, and things would crawl across me. And some of them I caught and ate, or maybe I dreamed that. I remember other things, in that swamp, like an organ that played a lot of the time, and sometimes angels in the air and devils in the water, but those were delirium, I guess.

Harley would say, "A little farther, Justin; we'll make it. And we'll get back at them, at all of them."

And we made it. We came to dry fields, cultivated fields with waist-high corn, but there weren't ears on the corn for me to eat. And then there was a stream, a clear stream that wasn't stinking water like the swamp, and Harley told me to wash myself and my clothes and I did, although I wanted to hurry on to where I could get food.

I still looked pretty bad; my clothes were clean of mud and filth but they were mere rags and wet, because I couldn't wait for them to dry, and I had a ragged beard and I was barefoot.

But we went on and came to a little farm building, just a two-room shack, and there was a smell of fresh bread just out of an oven, and I ran the last few yards to knock on the door. A woman, an ugly woman, opened the door and when she saw me she slammed it again before I could say a word.

Strength came to me from somewhere, maybe from Harley, although I can't remember him being there just then. There was a pile of kindling logs beside the door. I picked one of them up as though it were no heavier than a broomstick, and I broke down the door and killed the woman. She screamed a lot, but I killed her. Then I ate the hot fresh bread.

I watched from the window as I ate, and saw a man running across the field toward the house. I found a knife, and I killed him as he came in at the door. It was much better, killing with the knife; I liked it that way.

I ate more bread, and kept watching from all the windows, but no one else came. Then my stomach hurt from the hot bread I'd eaten and I had to lie down, doubled up, and when the hurting quit, I slept.

Harley woke me up, and it was dark. He said, "Let's get going; you should be far away from here before it's daylight."

I knew he was right, but I didn't hurry away. I was becoming, as you see, very clever now. I knew there were things to do first. I found matches and a lamp, and lighted the lamp. Then I hunted through the shack for everything I could use. I found clothes of the man, and they fitted me not too badly except that I had to turn up the cuffs of the trousers and the shirt. His shoes were big, but that was good because my feet were so swollen.

I found a razor and shaved; it took a long time because my hand wasn't steady, but I was very careful and didn't cut myself much.

I had to hunt hardest for their money, but I found it finally. It was sixty dollars.

And I took the knife, after I had sharpened it. It isn't fancy; just a bone-handled carving knife, but it's good steel. I'll show it to you, pretty soon now. It's had a lot of use.

Then we left and it was Harley who told me to stay away from the roads, and find railroad tracks. That was easy because we heard a train whistle far off in the night and knew which direction the tracks lay. From then on, with Harley helping, it's been easy.

You won't need the details from here. I mean, about the brakeman, and about the tramp we found asleep in the empty reefer, and about the near thing I had with the police in Richmond. I learned from that; I learned I mustn't talk to Harley when anybody else was around to hear. He hides himself from them; he's got a trick and they don't know he's there, and they think I'm funny in the head if I talk to him. But in Richmond I bought better clothes and got a haircut and a man I killed in an alley had forty dollars on him, so I had money again. I've done a lot of traveling since then. If you stop to think you'll know where I am right now.

I'm looking for Bull Mallon and the two men who helped him. Their names are Harry and Carl. I'm going to kill them when I find them. Harley keeps telling me that those fellows are big time and that I'm not ready for them yet. But I can be looking while I'm getting ready so I keep moving around. Sometimes I stay in one place long enough to hold a job as a printer for a while. I've learned a lot of things. I can hold a job and people don't think I'm too strange; they don't get scared when I look at them like they sometimes did a few months ago. And I've learned not to talk to Harley except in our own room and then only very quietly so people in the next room won't think I'm talking to myself.

And I've kept in practice with the knife. I've killed lots of people with it, mostly on the streets at night. Sometimes because they look like they might have money on them, but mostly just for practice and because I've come to like doing it. I'm really good with the knife by now. You'll hardly feel it.

But Harley tells me that kind of killing is easy and that it's something else to kill a person who's on guard, as Bull and Harry and Carl will be.

And that's the conversation that led to the bet I mentioned. I told Harley that I'd bet him that, right now, I could warn a man I was going to use the knife on him and even tell him why and approximately when, and that I could still kill him. And he bet me that I couldn't and he's going to lose that bet.

He's going to lose it because I'm warning you right now and you're not going to believe me. I'm betting that you're going to believe that this is just another story in a book. That you won't believe that this is the *only* copy of this book that contains this story and that this story is true. Even when I tell you how it was done, I don't think you'll really believe me.

You see I'm putting it over on Harley, winning the bet, by putting it over on you. He never thought, and you won't realize how easy it is for a good printer, who's been a counterfeiter too, to counterfeit one story in a book. Nothing like as hard as counterfeiting a five dollar bill.

I had to pick a book of short stories and I picked this one because I happened to notice that the last story in the book was titled *Don't Look Behind You* and that was going to be a good title for this. You'll see what I mean in a few minutes.

I'm lucky that the printing shop I'm working for now does book work and had a type face that matches the rest of this book. I had a little trouble matching the paper exactly, but I finally did and I've got it ready while I'm writing this. I'm writing this directly on a linotype, late at night in the shop where I'm working days. I even have the boss' permission, told him I was going to set up and print a story that a friend of mine had written, as a surprise for him, and that I'd melt the type metal back as soon as I'd printed one good copy.

When I finish writing this I'll make up the type in pages to match the rest of the book and I'll print it on the matching paper I have ready. I'll cut the new pages to fit and bind them in; you won't be able to tell the difference, even if a faint suspicion may cause you to look at it. Don't forget I made five and ten dollar bills you couldn't have told from the original, and this is kindergarten stuff compared to that job. And I've done enough bookbinding that I'll be able to take the last story out of the book and bind this one in instead of it and you won't be able to tell the difference no matter how closely you look. I'm going to do a perfect job of it if it takes me all night.

And tomorrow I'll go to some bookstore, or maybe a newsstand or even a drugstore that sells books and has other copies of this book, ordinary copies, and I'll plant this one there. I'll find myself a good place to watch from, and I'll be watching when you buy it.

The rest I can't tell you yet because it depends a lot on circumstances, whether you went right home with the book or what you did. I won't know till I follow you and keep watch till you read it—and I see that you're reading the last story in the book.

If you're home while you're reading this, maybe I'm in the house with you right now. Maybe I'm in this very room, hidden, waiting for you to finish the story. Maybe I'm watching through a window. Or maybe I'm sitting near you on the streetcar or train, if you're reading it there. Maybe I'm on the fire escape outside your hotel room. But wherever you're reading it, I'm near you, watching and waiting for you to finish. You can count on that.

You're pretty near the end now. You'll be finished in seconds and you'll close the book, still not believing. Or, if you haven't read the stories in order, maybe you'll turn back to start another story. If you do, you'll never finish it.

But don't look around; you'll be happier if you don't know, if you don't see the knife coming. When I kill people from behind they don't seem to mind so much.

Go on, just a few seconds or minutes, thinking this is just another story. Don't look behind you. Don't believe this—*until you feel the knife.*